Men and Angels

Elizabeth Cadell

The Friendly Air Publishing
thefriendlyairpublishing.com

This book is a work of fiction. Names, locals, business, organizations, and incidents are products of the author's imagination or are used fictitiously. Any resemblance to actual events, locals, or persons, living or dead, is entirely coincidental.

Copyright © 1952 by Elizabeth Cadell

This edition, Copyright © 2017 by the heirs of Elizabeth Cadell

"About the Author" Copyright © 2016 by Janet Reynolds

Cover art by Nikita Garets

All rights reserved.

No part of this book may be reproduced in any form or by any electronic or mechanical means, including information storage and retrieval systems, without written permission from the author, except for the use of brief quotations in a book review.

Chapter One

Rae Mansfield opened her eyes, turned over with a start to look at the alarm clock by her bed, and relaxed with a sigh of relief.

Sunday! She could stay in bed as long as she pleased. For the rest of the week, she must obey the clamorous alarm bell and prepare for a working day; on Sunday she could enjoy a leisurely, unhurried rising.

She stretched out her hand to the wireless set on the little table and, switching it on, lay listening to the strains of a dance band. Remembering the occupant of the other bedroom, she turned the volume down and relaxed comfortably, looking through the open door of her bedroom into the living-room beyond.

Her lips curved in amusement as she took in its disorder; Judy, she reflected, must have dressed last night in a greater hurry than usual. There was a blouse on the sofa, a skirt on the floor, shoes everywhere, two handbags, a plate with some crumbs on it.

Rae's eyes went to the open door opposite her own, and

she smiled more widely as she saw Judy's eiderdown on the floor and her blankets in a heap at the bottom of the bed. Sometimes, in cold weather, Rae would slip across and put the bedclothes on again—but this was May, and the air, though crisp, was not chilly enough to disturb the sleeper across the way. The narrow slit of sunshine across Rae's bed felt warm.

At the sight of the slit, her smile became a gurgle of laughter. Sunny aspect. Judy had been an easy victim; she had wanted this flat and had been only too willing to believe all that the agents said about it. She and Rae discovered, too late, that it had no sunny aspect and very few conveniences, but they had settled down and they were happy.

Over a year—it was hard to believe that time had gone so fast. It must be almost fourteen months—she had moved in on Judy's twentieth birthday.

A stir from the bed opposite brought Rae out of her reverie. She heard a moan and a yawn, loud, prolonged, and ending in a squeak.

"Rae?"

"Hm?"

"Awake?"

Rae slipped out of bed and walked across the living-room and into the bedroom opposite.

"What's the time?" asked Judy.

"Quarter-past ten. Hungry?"

"Oh, Lord, yes. I came in hungry, but I was too tired to

get anything."

"What are those crumbs?"

"Oh—those...I got a bit of something, but I was too tired to see. I was—Rae! Listen!"

The drowsiness banished from her eyes, Judy sat up with a jerk to listen to the low wailing coming from Rae's room. With a swoop, she turned on her own wireless as loud as it would go, and, lifting the set from the table, cradled it in her arms. The wailing rose to a heartbroken baying, and Judy listened with a look of ecstasy on her face.

"*—and I'll do-oo,*" promised the voice,

"*The same for you-oo*

Oh, my bew-oo-tiful Star of my Night."

The sound died away, the dance band blared once more. Judy, with a sigh, put the set back on the table.

"Isn't he *marvellous,* Rae?" she breathed.

Rae looked dubious.

"He's a bit stricken, isn't he?" she said slowly. "He never seems to—to cheer up."

"Of *course* not—that's his style, don't you see? He takes all his stuff at that slow, dragging rhythm—he makes every note *last.*"

"Well, isn't that because he gets paid by the minute? Why sing four songs if you can make two spin out?" asked Rae reasonably.

It was too early to be angry; Judy contented herself with a

look of scorn and settled back on her pillows.

Judy Ashton was small and dark, with beautiful eyes and hair so curly as to be unmanageable. Her skin was clear and smooth, and her rapid changes of expression gave her face an attractive vividness. When she spoke—and she was seldom silent—she looked like a child learning to dive—she took a deep breath, plunged, and then came up for air. Her manner with Rae, and with anyone she liked, was eager and affectionate, but to those who bored her, she showed an abruptness and rudeness bordering on insult. Nobody had succeeded in curing her of this regrettable tendency; Judy argued that she was under no obligation to be polite to anybody but her friends. Bores, she believed, could, like the wireless, be turned down or, better still, switched right off.

The two girls were strongly contrasted, both in looks and in character. Rae was taller and very fair; she was slender, quiet and restful. Her eyes, resting on Judy, held a good deal of humour. Her voice was low, and she spoke calmly and without emphasis.

A further contrast between the two lay in their circumstances. Judy's father had been a rich man, and had left each of his children comfortably off; Rae supported herself, and had no allowance to augment her salary. Judy dressed expensively; Rae spent far less, but was fortunate in possessing a figure on which ready-mades looked well. She walked to and from her work in Kingsway, while Judy was the possessor of a blue two-seater which was known to every bus-driver on the Baker

Street route.

Judy had followed Rae to London; she took occasional secretarial posts offered her by an agency. The flat was hers, and for some time Rae had refused to share it, for, in spite of its lack of amenities, it was central and therefore expensive. She had finally agreed to come upon her own terms; she would pay a nominal rent and cook the meals. Judy, eager to have her on any terms, gave in, and the arrangement had worked smoothly. The two girls got on well, and there was affection in Rae's eyes as she looked down at the tumbled figure on the bed.

"How did the party go last night?" she asked.

"It was all right," said Judy a shade doubtfully. "It would have been better if you'd been there, though."

"Well, I couldn't," pointed out Rae. "I couldn't have let Uncle Fabian down."

"Yes, you could, easily. It made our numbers uneven—Richard had got a man for you and, naturally, when you didn't turn up, he felt that someone owed him a bit of attention, so I had to spend half the evening convincing him it wasn't me."

"What did you do?"

"Dinner at that new place, and then on to dance. You should've been there, Rae—Richard's a wonderful dancer, considering he says he doesn't get any practice, and the others were pretty good—there were nine of us. You'd have made ten."

"Who were the others?"

"Nobody we've ever heard of—all Richard's Kenya crowd except this odd man, and he's from Kenya too, only Richard didn't know him out there—he met him on the boat coming home. He got on my nerves—he was one of those people who start off saying something, and as soon as they've got the general attention fixed on them, they dry up."

"Perhaps he's shy."

"Then he ought to go to a school for shys and get himself cured," said Judy. "Nobody's got time to sit and wait while he decides what it was he was going to say."

"How was your brother?"

"Richard? Oh, the same, only a bit thinner, I think. He thought I'd changed a lot—but three years makes more difference at my age. He looks older than twenty-six, but his manners haven't changed—he's still the same teasy sort. He can still get me irritated, but we got on well, on the whole. We went in pairs when we were young—Estelle and Bruce, and Richard and I—but two days in each other's company and Rich and I were fighting like Zulus—I wonder if you'll like him, Rae?"

"Does he look like his photographs?"

"Oh—those; well, yes. He's good-looking, but what I meant was, I wonder if you'll—well, fall for him. I wish you would."

Rae uncurled herself and stood up, smiling down at the dark, eager face.

"I wouldn't start match-making if I were you," she said in her slow, calm voice. "It never comes off. And this my-favourite-brother and my-best-friend is—"

"I know—it's the trickiest angle of all," said Judy. "I know that. But when I think things, I like to say them, and I'd be crazy, wouldn't I, if I didn't want you and Richard to fall in love?"

"You'd be crazy if you tried to make us," said Rae from the door. "Fried eggs and the week's bacon, or boiled with toast?"

"Any tomatoes?"

"No—oh yes. I got a pound, but at what a price...."

"Well, chuck 'em in and let's have a lovely fry. No liver or sausage or tiddly kidleys?"

"No."

"Pity. Oh, Rae—Richard came up last night."

"Up here?" Rae turned back, a little startled. "The place must have looked a shambles. I thought you were meeting him somewhere."

"I was, but he was in Baker Street and thought he'd come up. He came just as I was ironing my dress."

"Then I don't know how he got in at all," said Rae. "You always put the ironing board just in front of the door."

"Oh, he got in. But the first thing he did was to go round turning off the wirelesses. You'd left yours on in your bedroom, and my bedroom one was going and so was the big one, and he's one of those people who think you only ought to have it on when you want it. Who's got time to sit in front of the thing with the *Radio Times* in one hand and the switch in the other, putting it off and on?—Oh, and then he cleared the table."

"But I'd cleared it!"

"Yes, but I was hungry, so I'd made myself something. Then he put all my shoes in a row along the wall, so nice and neat. He'd make quite a husband, Rae."

"Good," said Rae. "I'll get the breakfast."

"Want any help?"

"No, not from you. Go and have a bath," advised Rae, "before the whole block gets up and runs off the hot water."

Judy got reluctantly out of bed and went into the bathroom. She gave a distasteful glance at the view—a series of back windows and fire escapes—and, sitting on the edge of the bath, turned on the hot-water tap and held her fingers under the flow.

"Cold!" she shouted indignantly. "Cold as Christmas, and it's not eleven yet. That's the fourth bath I haven't had on Sunday. Now I'll have to get up early to-morrow to get one, blast them."

"Too bad," said Rae from the kitchen. "Get the papers in, will you?"

"Yes—and oh, Rae, that reminds me. Richard's asked us to the theatre to-morrow night. I thought we might go and see that new show with Rosanna Lee in it—you know—Rose

Lewis that was."

"What sort of show is it?"

"What sort of show would it be, with Rosanna in it? Terrible, I bet. But it'd be interesting to see someone you've been at school with."

"I can't imagine Rose acting," commented Rae at the stove.

"She doesn't act. They say she stands there and recites her songs and gives the audience the idea that she could do much better, if only she could be bothered to try. And they like that, so she goes down quite well—let's go and see her."

"I don't mind," said Rae. "Put a cloth on the table, will you?"

Judy took a cloth from a drawer and threw it absently across the dining-table.

"How did *you* get on last night?" she asked.

Rae broke an egg neatly into the frying-pan.

"You won your bet," she said.

"*Honestly,* Rae? You mean, he didn't spend a sou?"

"Not one."

"But you must have—he must have. You can't spend an evening in London without spending money."

"Uncle Fabian can, and he can do it with—with grace, almost."

Judy came to the kitchen door and stood there, wide-eyed.

"What did you do?"

"The usual things. It's always the same routine with Uncle Fabian. A drive in the Park, a short stroll and then a drive home. Finished. But he was looking awfully handsome and—and debonair and young."

"Young! He's well over forty!"

"Not much over," said Rae, halving tomatoes neatly. "Nobody knows quite how old he is—he was much younger than my mother, and nobody on my father's side met him until he came to my mother's funeral."

"But why's he so mean, Rae? He isn't poor—you said yourself he's got a Rolls-Royce."

"He's got a nice comfortable income," said Rae calmly, "but there are lots of incomes which do very nicely for one, and which don't stretch to expensive favours for orphan nieces. I suppose, in a way, he does contribute something to society—he's tall and slim and beautifully dressed—he's exactly like those advertisements you see of figures standing in front of Tudor manors looking the picture of expensive ease. Nobody could look at him without pleasure."

"He must be as hard as nails. How does he come to have money, Rae, when your aunts lost all theirs?—I'm sorry if I'm poking my nose in."

"You're not. And he's nothing to do with my two aunts—they're my father's sisters. They thought that because my father was a good historian, he must be a good financier, too. They put all their money into the thing he advised them to put it into and then—"

"Wallop!"

"Yes. So it's just as well that Uncle Fabian's a bit hard, or he'd have been in the smash, too. He kept his money—and he's still keeping it."

There was silence for a time. Rae divided the breakfast into two equal platefuls and carried them to the table.

"Bring the coffee, will you?" she asked.

Judy carried in the coffee and poured out two cups. She handed one to Rae and looked at her in a puzzled way.

"If I'm nosey, then I'm nosey," she said, "but, Rae, this Uncle Fabian can't be as mean as all that. There was a general idea at Madame Soublin's—and it was spread by no less a person than Rosanna—that your uncle—that he—I mean, that he—"

"—paid my fees?" Rae smiled. "Well, he didn't. I don't suppose it's really amusing, but even my aunts can laugh at it now. They didn't then."

"Can you tell me—or is it a family secret or something?"

"It oughtn't to be exactly noised abroad," said Rae, "but I'll tell you, and then you won't waste any more time trying to make Uncle Fabian spend his money on me."

"Go on."

"Can I have another cup of coffee first?—Thanks. Well," began Rae, "I was fifteen when my father lost his money and sixteen when he died. I went to live with my aunts—"

"Hester and Anne?"

"Yes. The school I was at reduced the fees without being asked, so that wasn't a problem. Then I left and decided to take a job, and at that point Uncle Fabian paid us a visit and I met him for the first time. He was quite upset when he heard I was going out into the world—he said I was too young. A little finish—a little polish was necessary for a girl."

"And especially for his niece."

"Yes. My aunts said it was out of the question, and quite, quite unpractical. But Uncle Fabian talked them down, and lid that he would see a good scholastic agent and arrange it all."

"And pay it all?"

"Yes."

"But your aunts must have known the old so-and-so, after all. Didn't they suspect—"

"They suspected everything," said Rae. "He'd never been known to do a good deed before, and they knew that he kept getting entangled with young actresses—I know you don't believe that young ones would look at him, but then, you've never seen Uncle Fabian. While the aunts were busy suspecting, a letter came from Madame Soublin."

"I know," said Judy. "I saw the one she wrote Mother. The new, the up-to-date finishing school, uniting the social demands of the old world with the practical demands of the new. Cooking, dressmaking, typing—everything but washing-up—Wasn't that it?"

"Word for word. The fees sent both my aunts into a dead

faint, but when they recovered, they sold the next-to-last piece of family plate—it's quite true, they did—and fitted me out to be a credit to Madame Soublin."

"You were wonderful," said Judy, eyes half closed in reminiscence. "I'll never forget the first time I saw you—you came up the green corridor with Madame—she all bounce and bosom, and you gliding behind like a pale lily in that débutante-sports affair—remember?"

"I remember," smiled Rae. "I thought I was going to hate it—and how we all loved it! Two years of heaven."

"Two years—but where were the fees?" enquired Judy, returning to practical matters.

"That's exactly the way Madame Soublin put it. Where were the fees? My aunts had no idea, but when they got in touch with Uncle Fabian, they didn't waste much time hoping, because he was—"

"Young actresses?"

"Yes. My aunts said nothing to me for over a year, and they scraped and scraped and—I know," said Rae slowly, "that you think that they're just two ordinary, rather plain people, but I think they're wonderful."

"So do I. If they hadn't paid the fees, you wouldn't have stayed and then we'd never have met. But, Rae, to come back to your Uncle Fabian; what actress would go out with him just to get a drive round the Park?"

"They don't understand the situation just at first," explained Rae. "He looks so expensive that they're misled. But then it gradually—"

"—dawns on them—why d'you go out with him, Rae? Why don't you just cut him right out?"

"Sentiment, I suppose," said Rae thoughtfully. "He's my only relation on my mother's side, and I always imagine she would have liked me to bear with him. I don't expect anything from him, so I never feel disappointed—he even spoke of paying my rent here."

"But he only spoke!"

"Yes. Then he talked of my keeping house for him, but by that time I knew pretty well what he was, and so I didn't take it seriously. I'm sorry for him, in a way. ... If you'll help me out with these things, I'll wash them up."

"And I'll ring up and tell Richard about tomorrow night. We'll go to this show of Rosanna's. And, Rae—you will try to like him, won't you? It's funny to say complimentary things about one's own brother, but he really is marvellous—will you try?"

"If he's marvellous," said Rae, with her accustomed calmness, "then I shan't have to try."

Chapter Two

Rae dressed carefully for the theatre party on the following night. She wanted to look well, but not too well; she wanted to make an effort to attract Richard Ashton, but she did not want to make the effort apparent to Judy. She had met Judy's suggestions, she considered, with a subduing degree of coolness. Judy was a darling, but she was—in this matter—too open to be encouraged.

Rae knew a great deal about Richard Ashton. She had lived for over a year with his photograph, which represented him as a dark, handsome, somewhat commanding young man. She had listened to long extracts from his letters to Judy, and had built up a picturesque, if inaccurate, background of Kenya farms, African lions and elephant hunts, interspersed with pleasant visits to Nairobi. She knew that he was given to teasing, that he was popular with both men and women; she knew that he had declared himself to be heartwhole, and had instructed his sister to find him a wife. Rae—like Judy—was of the opinion that he could go much farther and fare much worse, but she was more sensitive than Judy and a good deal more shy. If Richard Ashton showed any signs of liking her, decided Rae, putting the last touches to her make-up, she would be willing to respond; this evening would show whether there was going to be anything to respond to.

It was a cheerless evening for a first meeting; rain fell heavily as Rae and Judy, sheltering under the porter's umbrella, hurried from their door to the little blue car waiting at the pavement's edge. Before Rae had opened the door on the other side, her hair was disordered and her thin shoes wet. She gathered the heavy folds of her dress round her, and Judy drove out of the side-road into the traffic of Baker Street.

"We're late," she commented. "It's just as well I told Richard we'd meet him at the theatre."

"What's the other man's name?" asked Rae.

"Clarke. No—Peake. No, not Peake, but something short like that. I didn't think we needed a fourth—you and I and Richard could've had a nice threesome, but he said it looked unbalanced, so now this Peake or Whoever is coming, and he'll be just as superfluous as he was the other evening—gosh, Rae, did you *see* that bit of driving? He scraped me by a hair."

"I thought you scraped him."

"Well, he ought to have moved. Can you wipe your window? I can't see a thing. I'm not looking forward to this party much. You'll talk to Richard and I'll have to devote myself to—I wish I could think of his name. Perhaps it's Deane. I seem to remember calling him Deane, but his conversation wasn't the kind that keeps you on your toes, exactly. What he does get out—after an effort—isn't worth answering. He brought up the

Men and Angels

war, and talked as though I'd never heard of it. When he said 'But you're too young to remember' for the fifth time, I made an effort and told him that I knew all about it, because I'd been machine-gunned on a beach when I was at school, and if that wasn't war, what was? So he came down a couple of octaves and—*What* did that vanman say, Rae?"

"Well, I missed the actual—"

"So did I," said Judy regretfully. "I wish he'd shouted it a bit louder—I'm certain it was one I hadn't heard before. Is it this turning for that garage, or the next? I think— Hell! wouldn't you think people would signal before they shoot in front of you like that?—Here we are. No, I don't have to take her in—the man does that. Come on, Rae—we've got to scoot."

Scooting, the girls reached the theatre to find the crowd in the foyer thinning. Judy looked from side to side in search of her brother.

"There they are," she said. "What d'you think of him, Rae?—D'you think he looks nice?"

There was not very much time for Rae to make up her mind on the subject. She watched Richard Ashton and his companion walking towards them, and knew only that he was as tall and as good-looking as she had imagined. His voice was pleasant, but his greeting was brief; introducing his friend merely as 'Edward', he led the party with scarcely any pause to their seats; the lights were lowered almost immediately and the orchestra broke into a noisy overture. Speech was impossible, and Rae settled herself to await the rising of the curtain.

The revue was not one of the current successes, and Rae found its humour a little broad. She was of a generation which thought nothing shocking except an ignorance of what was called Life, but she had drawn for herself a line between what she thought funny and what was slightly distasteful. She enjoyed the feeling of being close to Richard, and her interest in the stage only revived with the entrance of Rosanna Lee.

Miss Lee walked slowly on to an empty stage, leaned in an effective manner against a backcloth representing a café, and sang a dirge about a girl whose lover had failed to keep an appointment. Rae, endeavouring to form an unbiased opinion, came to the conclusion that there was nothing in the performance which she could not have done equally well herself. Rosanna had, so far as she could see, no talent, no voice, and not a great deal of personality, but she agreed that there was a strong suggestion that the singer was holding something back. The applause was enthusiastic enough to allow Rosanna to come back twice and give a tired little droop before making way for an underclad chorus.

The curtain dropped after the first half of the show and Richard turned to smile at Rae.

"How?" he asked.

"It's got a lot of colour," said Rae cautiously.

"And did you understand all the allusions?"

"Yes."

"Good. You can put me right—half of them went over my

head. That's the worst of living out of London—drink?"

"Thank you."

"How about you, Judy?" asked Richard. "Coming or staying?"

Judy's preference was written plainly upon her face for all to read, but her first eager assent was quenched by a feeling that she ought to let Rae and Richard go out alone. A side-glance at the thin, long-faced man beside her, however, obviously convinced her that ten minutes of his unadulterated company would be insupportable.

"We're coming," she said.

Rae always accepted the first drink she was offered; as she never drank it, the label made little difference. She had tried earnestly to accustom herself to even the mildest of cocktails, and had found that they gave her a sensation of mingled sleepiness and sickness and ruined what small conversational powers she possessed. When Judy was with her, she was at ease, for Judy, on whom the most shattering mixtures had no effect whatsoever, substituted her empty glass for Rae's full one.

The four stood holding their drinks at one end of the bar, talking as well as the jostling crowd round them would permit. Judy made a strong effort to interest herself in Edward's conversation, and Richard was free to talk to Rae. He looked at her with an unembarrassed scrutiny as he talked; she was his sister's closest friend, and he evidently saw no reason for concealing his interest.

"How do you like living with Judy?" he asked.

"Oh"—Rae smiled—"it seems to work very well."

"It ought to," he said. "You're a well-contrasted pair—she can do all the talking while you have all the ideas. Does she do her share of the washing-up?"

"No."

"Ah! You do the lot?"

"Not quite. It's on a business basis," explained Rae in her level tones. "She pays more, I do more. The rent—even half of it—was a bit out of my reach."

"Surprise Number One," said Richard. "You're like one of these quietly opulent girls."

"I'm only quiet."

"You can't be too quiet if you understood all those offside jokes they were giving out—what did you think of your old schoolmate?"

"Rosanna? I—well, it seems a bit difficult to see how she —how—"

"How she ever persuaded anybody to give her a bit part?"

"Yes. She isn't really—I don't say that I could do any better, but—"

"But all the same, you're pretty sure you could. Surprise Number Two. I felt sure you'd be the generous, loyal type."

In spite of the lazy casualness of his manner, Rae felt herself stung to self-defence.

"I'm a little prejudiced," she said. "She used to borrow my

clothes without asking—and my wardrobe wasn't really built to accommodate two."

"Borrow? But she looks half your size!"

"She is—but she thought nothing of taking in a sizable tuck or two wherever it was needed. You had to do quite a lot of dressmaking when you eventually got the garments back."

"I can see that would sour a girl," said Richard. "Why didn't she borrow Judy's?"

"Because she did it once and I made her see that once was too many," said Judy, glad to abandon Edward. "She didn't do it any more. But Rae can't tread on people's faces, and so she gets put upon. She needs protection—hey! What d'you think you're doing?"

"Protecting her," said Richard, tightening his grasp on her wrist. "Is that, or is it not Rae's drink?"

" 'Course it's Rae's. Lemme go—I'm going to drink it. I don't do this because I want the stuff, but because—oh, there's the *bell*, Richard—let me *go*!"

"Sure you don't want it?" Richard asked Rae, his grip still firm.

"Quite sure, thanks."

Richard released his sister and shepherded the party back to their seats.

"Next time I ask you to have one," he asked Rae, "do I drink it myself?"

"Yes, please."

Richard's voice came in a low murmur through the darkness.

"A grand girl to take out," he said. "When shall we begin?"

They began immediately after the show. Standing outside the theatre, they discussed the relative merits of a restaurant or a night club.

"What do you think, Edward?" asked Richard.

Edward, thus publicly appealed to, found himself bereft of the half-dozen suggestions which had passed through his mind only a moment ago.

"Well, I really don't" he began, and stopped. "What I was going to suggest—"

Judy looked at him with an exaggerated expectancy that did nothing to help him.

"You were saying?" she asked politely.

"Yes. Never get it out," explained Edward.

"We've got all night," said Judy. "And all tomorrow and all—"

"Shut up, Judy," said Richard.

"Oh no, don't," implored Edward. "My mother used to do the—She used to get just like Judy and—No, I mean, do go on."

"We're waiting to," said Judy. "The point is, where do we go on to?"

"Heard of a place, once. Can't call it to—Well, perhaps. Yes. The Waterside."

"The Waterside, then," said Richard.

"No." Judy spoke decisively. "I don't like night clubs much, anyway, but that one's out—Rosanna goes on there after the theatre and does a turn—and I'm not going to sit through Rosanna twice in one evening. What's wrong with a restaurant? I'm hungry—let's just go somewhere and *eat*."

They went, Rae and Richard in a taxi, Edward in Judy's little car. He was noticeably paler when he arrived at the restaurant, but the experience seemed to have increased his obvious admiration for Judy. Undaunted by her inattention, he made several attempts throughout the meal to complete a sentence, without, however, much success. He began well—he leaned forward and got out his first few words with ease and fluency, but before the subject matter could be learnt, the sound of his own voice had frightened him into silence. Rae, watching—for the first time—a human being quite unmoved by Judy's incivility, found herself liking him more and more. His bland indifference, even when Judy subjected him to what she termed the deep-freeze, made her feel that there was a good deal more in him than he allowed to appear. Richard watched him appreciatively and turned to Rae with a smile.

"He's a wonderful fellow," he said, as though Edward were not present. "Know what he did on board? Got permission to hold a children's party on his birthday—to celebrate his quarter-century. The steward put up a wonderful tea and Edward provided some of Simon Arzt's best toys. He made us line all the kids up on the upper deck while—"

"Before tea," put in Edward.

"That's it—he got us to line them up just before tea to watch Father Neptune coming on board with the toys. Then young Edward—dressed as Father Neptune—clambers up, nice and wet, from the lower deck and—"

There was a tearing sound; Rae and Judy, looking up in alarm, identified it as Edward's laugh.

"Good disguise," he chuckled.

"Too good," proceeded Richard. "It might have been the Old Man of the Sea in person—dripping seaweed, clutching his trident, sea-green whiskers...."

"The children must have loved it," said Rae.

"You think so? The children," said Richard, "gave one combined scream and threw several combined fits. They were all taken to their cabins and given sedatives, and their parents spent the rest of the voyage telling Edward what they thought of him."

"Good tea," commented Edward.

"Yes, we enjoyed that, I must say—let's eat something now."

Judy discovered that Edward could not only translate the menu into English, but could also tell her what each dish was composed of. After watching the two in unexpectedly amicable conversation, Richard turned to Rae.

"Does Judy have to eat your food for you, too?" he asked.

"No—I can do that pretty well, thanks—how do you find

England?"

"England? Oh, mine's only a tourist's view now, I'm afraid. I see the changes, but nothing touches me too closely. People grumble, but then, people always did. It's difficult to get them off the subject of food, but that's not altogether the result of the new conditions, either. I had an Aunt Jane who used to travel extensively in the old, old days—long before your time—and all she ever talked about when she got back was the good food you got in the Hotel This, or the bad food you got in the Hotel That. Snow on a mountain reminded her of thick cream on her trifle; rivers were gravy, and sunsets were strawberry and vanilla ices—thick soup, or the watery kind?"

"Thick, please—unless they've got that nice cold jelly kind."

"How like Aunt Jane—they have. And to follow, as they say? What do you think should have the privilege of following the iced soup down that so-slender throat?"

He spoke in the half-bantering tone he habitually used, and Judy spoke impulsively.

"Richard, you're not to tease her. She isn't used to it."

"She will be. What," asked Richard, "are you two doing about holidays?"

"Holidays? You mean, when're we taking them?"

"Yes. When, where and for how long?"

"I can go away when I like," said Judy. "Rae can't, though—and I shan't be free in June, because I told the Agency

I'd take a job down at Allbrook."

"The Allbrook six miles from Thorpe?" asked Richard.

"Yes. I thought it might be nice to be near home—I could run over to Thorpe and see Mother now and again."

"What's the job?" asked Richard.

"Secretary to a sort of Summer School for Art students—one of these London Art Schools has rented Allbrook Grange. I've got to live in—I don't fancy living on the job, but if I get fed up I can always have a night or two at home, and anyhow, I'd have week-ends there. And there's another thing—they've got a lot of well-known artists going down to run the school and Aylmer Ferris is going to be down there the whole time. I thought it would be nice if I got him to do a portrait of Mother; if he agreed, I could drive him over at week-ends. He's one of the best-known portrait painters in the country, and if he'd do a portrait of Mother at his lowest terms, I'd give it to you to take back to Kenya. Would you like that?"

"I can only tell you," said Richard, "when I've seen the portrait. Do I have to pay for it? If it's for me, I'd like to see what the fellow's doing."

"Well, but you can't. You won't be there."

"I've got to spend some time at home," said Richard, "and I've got an even better idea than yours."

Judy looked surprised.

"Well, what?"

Richard turned to Rae.

Men and Angels

"Tell me," he asked, "when do *you* do your summer schooling?"

"Me? I—well, I only get a fortnight," said Rae. "With luck, three weeks, and I have to take it when the man I work for takes his."

"And is there any chance of his taking it in June?"

"He m-might," said Rae, stammering a little in her efforts to see where the questions were leading. "Why?"

"Why don't you come and spend the three weeks at home?" asked Richard. "I'd have my grey export drophead coupé by then—that's point one. Two, home's a bit on the lonely side—it's—"

"Rae, you *couldn't!*" brought out Judy slowly and reluctantly. "Honestly, you couldn't. Richard, she *couldn't!*"

"Tell her why," invited Richard, settling down to his plate of food. "I'll listen."

Judy looked at Rae.

"I'd love you to go," she said slowly, "and with Richard there, perhaps—well, it might be different, but you see, there's nothing to *do* at Thorpe. When there were four of us there for school holidays, it was marvellous—a nice big house, huge grounds, and nobody for miles—we had wonderful times—didn't we, Rich?"

"We did," said Richard. "And we could again."

"No, you couldn't," persisted Judy. "Everything's quite different now. You can't ask Rae down just as if you were invit-

31

ing her to an ordinary house in the country."

"What's extraordinary about it?" asked Richard.

"Everything. You may as well know, Rae, what you're in for. It's lovely country, but it *is* country, and none of your bus services or easy hops into Town. You can get there, and then you have to stay there. The nearest thing to our house is a farm, and that's over two miles away. And Mother's a darling, and there's nothing really wrong with old Uncle Bertram, once you get used to him—and there's quite a nice normal woman who's a friend of Mother's—she's called Miss Beckwith. Just those three. Uncle Bertram comes out now and again, because he belongs to a Club in London, but the other two—Mother and Miss Beckwith—live down there and never move. Mother does the cooking, and when she's finished one day's meals, she sits down and plots out the next; Miss Beckwith glides round the house counting linen and making beds, and they both feel that the bees have nothing on them. They don't even listen to the wireless—Uncle Bertram listens to the News every night and keeps them in touch with anything that's going on—not that they care, but they wouldn't like people to know. They've shut themselves up in a nice little cocoon; the house is like a church, it's so quiet, and when you go there you step out of life into a sort of—of backwater. It doesn't worry me—or Richard, or the others. We go down armed with wirelesses and the latest novels and some new records, and we manage. But we don't take people down any more—it's like throwing a brick into a duckpond," said Judy.

Men and Angels

"Where's the harm in chucking a brick in a duckpond?" asked Richard. "It's a harmless sort of amusement."

"You still haven't answered," said Judy. "What's the use of landing Rae in a place like Thorpe? What'll you do?"

Richard finished a mouthful, pushed his plate aside and turned to Rae.

"I'll tell you," he said. "I'll take you up to the three attics, where all our old treasures are stored. I'll take you through the woods and show you all the bunny-holes. We'll swim in our quite private pool, and we'll sunbathe on its banks. I'll show you the arbour we built—all by ourselves, in stone. I'll drive you up and down our hilly roads—only thirty miles from this table and yet so quiet, so unpeopled, so lonely and so peaceful. We'll go out in the morning and come back late at night. I'll show you our Duchess, if she's still alive; I'll show you our tree-house. Don't let Judy frighten you—I'll provide all the entertainment—how about it? Will you come?"

There was a moment's pause.

"Yes, I'll come," said Rae quietly.

She would go. If it meant holding her chief up at pistol point, if it meant throwing up her job—she would go. She would go more than thirty miles to be near that tall, strong form and listen to the low, teasing voice. He was completely unreadable; she had no means of knowing whether he wanted her as a companion, or whether he was using her to hold off the boredom of a spell of home life. She had no idea what he thought of her. She had come out with childish plans for subjugating Judy's brother, and she had met an unexpectedly mature man of the world whose provocative, elusive manner must have baffled many older and wiser women. He was only twenty-six, but he appeared years older than the men of the same age with whom she had dined and danced. He had the assurance of thirty and the ease of forty. She had assumed that her friendship with Judy would place her at once on an easy footing with her brother; instead, he had talked down to her and made her feel as though she was still in the shell.

She looked up and found his eyes on her with what she feared was amusement.

"I've just had the most wonderful idea," he said. "Want to hear it?"

"No," said Edward.

"You've guessed it," said Richard. "I'm going to let you pay the bill."

Chapter Three

There was a great deal to be done before May came to an end. Richard, after a brief visit to his mother at Thorpe, went up to Liverpool on business; Judy joined the London headquarters of the Art School, and began to work on the arrangements for the move to Allbrook. Rae had to tell her aunts that she would not be spending her holiday with them, and she had also to interview her employer with a view to finding out whether she could have the holiday at all.

Matters went more easily than she had expected. She spent a restless night composing sentences to be delivered in a firm voice at her office:

'I should very much like, Mr. Marshall, to be free for the last three weeks of June.'

'I take it, Mr. Marshall, that you've no objection to my taking my fortnight's holiday in June? It would suit me very well if you could arrange your Directors' Meetings so as to allow me three consecutive weeks.'

'I'm sorry, Mr. Marshall—my plans are quite complete.'

'In that case, Mr. Marshall, I'm very sorry, but—'

'I repeat, Mr. Marshall—the last three weeks in June—'

It was very convincing during the night, but on the following morning Rae felt that she would be unable to conduct the interview on firm lines. She would stammer and make ineffectual attempts to put the matter boldly, but it would end in his being irritated and in her giving notice for she was determined to go to Thorpe, and no Mr. Marshall, she resolved, was going to stop her.

No interview of any kind was necessary, however, for what Rae regarded as the kindest, the most benevolent Providence struck Mr. Marshall down with an attack of jaundice; he was ordered to bed and, since Rae's duties were connected solely with his affairs, the firm advised her to take her holiday during his absence.

So much was over. The aunts still remained, and Rae journeyed to Bath for a week-end to explain that she was spending three weeks at Judy's home. The aunts were very pleased; if they suspected that there was a young man in the case, they expressed no hopes and uttered no warnings.

"What," enquired Aunt Hester, "are you going to do with the flat while you and Judy are away?"

Rae looked at her in surprise.

"Do? Well, we hadn't thought—I mean, we were just going to leave it." The surprise gave way to a new thought. "Look, Aunt Hester, why don't you both go up and stay in it while we're away? You can do shopping, and theatres and—"

"That wasn't quite the idea," said Aunt Hester. "It occurred to me that if you're going to leave the place empty for three weeks—"

"Oh, but there's a caretaker and everything," said Rae. "He—"

"Splendid. But it's always well to wait until a person finishes a sentence—then you know what they're trying to say."

"Sorry, Auntie."

"As I say, it struck me that if you're going to leave the place empty for three weeks, it would be a good opportunity for us to go up and give it a good going-over."

"Who's 'us'?" enquired Aunt Anne anxiously.

"You and me. It'll require all of three weeks' hard work from two people—you and me—to remove the accumulation of filth that those two girls have—"

"*Filth*, Auntie?"

"—that those two girls have lived in for the past year. The last time I went up, the bag of the vacuum-cleaner had a split in it, and the dust came out as fast as it went in."

"We ordered a new bag, Auntie."

"And has it come?"

"Well, no—not yet, but—"

"Have you ever taken the things down that were thrown on that tall cupboard?"

"No, Auntie. We—"

"How often have you had the rugs up?"

"Well, we—"

"When did you last scrub the larder shelves?"

"As a matter of—"

"Or dust the bookshelves?"

"We—"

"And when did you last have the curtains down, or the blankets washed, or the sink-boards scrubbed or the lamp-shades dusted and the—"

"I think, Hester," broke in Aunt Anne, "that while you're at the flat, I'll run up and spend some time with poor—"

"Poor nothing," said Aunt Hester. "The place is a pigsty. We shall go up and give it a thorough do."

Rae reported this conversation to Judy, who looked round the flat with a new curiosity.

"Pigsty?"

"Yes, it is," said Rae. "They're quite right. When we come back, it'll all smell of strong soap and wax polish.

"We'd better clear some of the accumulation of papers and rubbish out of those drawers."

The clearing disclosed a great deal of unanswered correspondence, Accounts Rendered, crumpled paper patterns and a miscellany of snapshots.

"Golly!" Judy, abandoning all attempts at tidying, sat cross-legged on the floor, turned up the wireless, and settled down to a happy session with the photographs. "Look—there's you that day down at Rottingdean, and—"

Men and Angels

"I can't *hear*," said Rae.

Judy repeated the information in a loud voice, and the conversation continued over the strident sounds issuing from the radio. They had no thought of turning it down; noise was their natural background, confusion their natural element. They rose to music, dressed to two programmes going simultaneously and thought silence uncanny. Papers accumulated round Rae as she sat sorting and tearing.

"Whose card is that you've just torn up?" asked Judy.

"Uncle Fabian's. He never writes when he invites you. He just sends his card with the time and place written on the back and a pretty little bit like: 'May I have the pleasure?' or 'I do so hope you can come.' "

"And then you go and all you get's a drive. Honestly, Rae, I don't see how you can be right about *girls* going about with him. He might be good-looking, or even young-looking—I don't say he isn't, but can you see *me,* for instance, going round with a man of forty whatisit?"

"With this one, yes," said Rae. "If he weren't my uncle, and if I didn't know how really mean he is, I could enjoy being with him."

"What—you mean even if you had the chance of going out with someone young? I don't believe it."

Rae gave up the attempt to explain her uncle's success with girls. It would be impossible to tell Judy that charm was ageless, and that when Fabian Hollis was fifty, sixty and more, he would still attract with his air of breeding, his unusual good looks, his wit and knowledge of the world. In time, she knew, girls tired of him. Wit and charm were all very well, but so were theatres and dances and dinners, none of which Fabian provided. More was expected from a man with a Rolls-Royce than drives in the Park. When it became obvious that no more was forthcoming, it was natural that girls would look for something more practical than polish.

Richard returned from Liverpool early in June and rang Rae up at her office.

"How long is the day?" he enquired without preamble.

"You mean—"

"Quite so," said Richard. "Five or five-thirty?"

"Half-past, I'm afraid."

"My God!" said Richard. "Haven't you got a Union? How about a nice dark cinema with a nice light dinner afterwards?"

"Thank you very much."

"Thank you very much yes, or thank you very much no?"

"I'd like to come, thank you," said Rae.

"Don't sound so prim. Say 'Yeah, that's a date.' Haven't you got any cross-talk?"

"Well, no," said Rae.

"Ah!" The tone, light and teasing, brought him vividly before her; she could almost see the provocative expression in his eyes. "Ah! You're the slow one. How do I pick you out from all the other typists when you come out of the cage?"

Men and Angels

"I'm in black," said Rae.

"Black. And what are all the others in?"

"Well, they're in black, too."

"That's the end," said Richard, and rang off.

Rae spent a good deal of the rest of the afternoon in the washroom, trying to do something with her hair, which before the telephone call had seemed the picture of perfection. After doing it four times, she decided it would have to stay as it was. She washed her face and made it up slowly and carefully, wishing she had some of Judy's dark, pretty colouring. Blondes were all very well, but they lacked sparkle—and Richard seemed to expect sparkle.

She went back to her typewriter and stared at the keys. She was feeling a little confused. The familiar objects on her desk had an odd look, as though they were far away instead of at her elbow. The white letters on Mr. Marshall's door looked misty and the figures in the main office seemed to be moving slowly and heavily instead of with their usual scuttling haste. Everything was vague—until she thought of Richard Ashton.

Rae took out her handkerchief and rubbed her palms, which felt moist. The tired feeling which had weighed on her for the past hour seemed to increase, and at last she pushed her work aside, examined her symptoms and confronted the question which she would have much rather avoided: Was she, or was she not, falling in love?

If she was, she decided, she was doing it in rather a hurry.

She had thought—and talked—a great deal about love, but her position, in her dreams, had always been a very strong one. It had been one of cautious deliberation; should she, or should she not, return the affection which was being laid at her feet? That was all a girl had to do—make up her mind. The man fell in love, the man wooed, the man hoped, the man waited—all a girl had to do was to take her time and be sure it was not just excitement and the size of the sapphire.

Fighting down a feeling of panic, she reviewed her position. She was falling—she had fallen—in love with Richard Ashton. She had seen his handsome likeness every day in the flat for the past year; she had discussed him with Judy; she had allowed Judy to bring them together in an undisguisedly hopeful way; she had met him, and she had behaved like an unsophisticated schoolgirl. If he had asked her, an hour ago, to go to Ceylon instead of to the cinema, she would have said yes with the same meek, obvious alacrity.

The door with the white letters opened, and it became imperative to put love in its place. Rae worked hard for the next two hours and found herself steadier at the end of it. Falling in love before being encouraged was unwise, she acknowledged, but perhaps the encouragement would follow.

She was relieved to find that some certainly followed over dinner. Richard, now in possession of his export model drove her to a riverside restaurant and ordered the meal without any reference to her whatsoever; he watched her as she drank, under his orders, a whole glass of wine, and allowed her to sleep it off against his shoulder in the car. He drove home slowly, putting one of her hands on the wheel and his own firmly over hers. Arrived at her door, and oblivious to the unconcealed interest of the hall porter, he explained that he always kissed a girl after taking her out, in case she felt under any obligation. When he raised his head, Rae had to admit, a little breathlessly, that all sense of obligation was gone.

The porter took her up in the lift, merely remarking that it was a fine night for that sort of thing. And the street, he ended less cordially as he took the lift down, a fine place.

Rae opened the door of the flat and went in slowly, making a mental summary of the evening. Her sense of humour, for some reason—perhaps, she thought, the wine—seemed to be in better working order. The grim thought of loving, unloved, had lost its sting. She had begun the evening with some vague ideas of being more distant, less amenable. Well, she hadn't been amenable; she had merely behaved as any intelligent lamb would behave when an eagle swooped down and got its claws round it. Frightening, yes, but worth it for the wonderful feeling of being born up into the sky.

Judy was undressing—she had one half of her pyjamas on, and was conducting an energetic search under the sofa for the other—and in Rae's eyes, the more important half. A glimpse of pink silk behind the wireless table caught the searcher's eye.

"Oh, *there*! Thanks—who've you been out with, Rae?" she asked with her customary directness.

"Richard. Flicks and dinner."

"Oh! Was he nice?"

"He's your brother," said Rae. "Don't you know?"

"I mean, did he *try* anything," persisted Judy. "Did he just say good night, or did he spin it out?"

"Ring him up," invited Rae, "and ask him."

"Oh, Rae, don't be *silly,*" said Judy, still on the floor. "I'm *interested,* can't you see? Richard would tell me to go to hell, and if *you're* going to be uncommunicative, then how'm I to know anything at all? I want him to *like* you, and I want you to like *him,* and when you get together I want to know what you do. I don't mean what you *do,* exactly, but how things are going. This isn't just indelicate curiosity, it's an honest desire for knowledge. If you don't like him, then say so, and I won't mind—I'll be a bit surprised, because after all, girls *do* fall down like ninepins when Richard gets among them, but if you don't get along with him, then you just don't, only I can't just sit here knowing nothing, can I, and you just saying nothing until right at the end, if there *is* any end. Oh, Rae, go on—tell me!"

"It *is* indelicate curiosity," said Rae. "I like him—and that's really all. I haven't the faintest—not the smallest, smallest idea what he thinks of me. I don't know what he thinks of anything—his feelings are where I suppose everybody's feeling should be—inside. If he ever falls in love with me, and if he lets me know, I'll let you know. Is that all right?"

"It'll have to be, I suppose," grumbled Judy. "I wondered all the evening whether you'd gone out with him. I had a terrible time here."

"Why?"

"That Edward came. He was clutching orchids in cellophane, and could he get out who they were for? Not him. I put him on the wobbly chair, hoping he'd go soon, but no. I looked at the orchids and said, 'Shall I put them down?' but no. I said 'Coffee?' but no."

"Was the wireless going as loud as that?"

"I don't know—I suppose so. Gosh! I forgot to turn it down—but it doesn't matter. That flat opposite is still empty. Is it midnight?"

"Past." Rae lowered the volume. "When did he go?"

"Edward? I didn't notice. I wasn't going to sit and do a monologue for an unspecified number of hours. I showed him how the door opened, and then I went and washed a blouse and some stockings. When I came back, nothing. Oh, and *who* d'you think rang up? It's no use—you'll never guess. Rosanna. Rosanna Lee, no less. She said Helloo, Judy'—just as she used to, remember? And I said 'Rose darling, I saw your show the other night and you were *terrible!*'"

"Oh, Judy—you didn't!"

"Why not? She was. She agreed she was, but she says she gets forty pounds a week for being it. For-ty pounds a *week*— for that!"

"Good heavens," said Rae, in equal amazement. "What did she ring up for?"

"To ask us to a party—imagine! You and me at a party with all those peculiarities in that show. It's her birthday—she's got hold of eight ex-Madame Soublin's—you and me and the Mount twins and I forget who else. The only thing is, we can't go. It's the Thursday after we go away—I'll be in this collection of artists, and I must say they get funnier every time I look at them—and you'll be at Thorpe."

Rae yawned. A party of Rosanna's was nothing to regret.

"Hope I can get up in the morning," she said sleepily. "'Night." She gave a glance round the room. "Judy?"

"Hm?"

"Where are the orchids?"

Judy, wide-eyed, turned her head this way and that and peered under the chairs.

"Gone!" she exclaimed in astonishment. "He must have bought them on approval!"

Rae frowned and spoke hesitatingly.

"I wish you wouldn't treat people like that, Judy," she said.

"Like what?"

"Well—so rudely."

Judy leaned back on her hands and looked up in silence for some moments.

"Look," she said at last. "You say it's rude. A man comes

Men and Angels

here prepared to spend the whole evening cosily, and I won't play—and you say that's rude."

"Yes, it *is* rude. You could be a bit frigid, perhaps, or you could show him in some way that you—"

"With his kind," stated Judy, "there isn't any other way. Look at it like this: did he come here tonight for his own satisfaction or for mine? No, don't argue—just say."

"Well, for his, I suppose."

"All right. He's got a few hours on his hands, so he says, 'I know what I'll do—I'll look up those girls, and that'll pass the time nicely till dinner.' *He's* got nothing to do, and so *I've* got to put aside all the things I'm dying to do, just to fill in his time—is that it?"

"He merely pays a pleasant—"

"He merely wants his time filled in, and I showed him he couldn't fill it in here. When you don't like people, Rae, I watch you—it takes you four perfectly good evenings to do what I've just done in one. What's rude about it? You wouldn't have said it was rude if our footman, which we haven't got, had shoved a caller's hat back in his hand and said 'Not at home'—would you? Well, we've got no protection of that sort now, so we make our own. Good heavens, Rae, I've hardly got time to fit in people I *like*—why should this Edward, who's got a whole leave to fill in, fill it in in our drawing-room? Consider—if you'd been here, you'd have been sweet to him and he'd have taken root with his orchids on our doorstep. Would you have liked that?"

"No, I wouldn't."

"There you are, then," said Judy. "That's what I've saved us from."

Chapter Four

There were only four days left before Richard's departure for Thorpe. He was to go on Saturday; Judy would leave the flat on Friday, spend the night at the newly opened Summer School at Allbrook and meet Richard at Thorpe on Saturday for the week-end. Rae was to go down on Monday—Richard had pressed her to go earlier, but she had refused—she felt it better to let the family have a week-end without strangers, and she was also anxious to settle her aunts into the flat before she left.

She went out with Richard on three successive nights; he parted from her each evening without any arrangements for another meeting, and rang her up at the office the next day. When he rang up on Friday, however, she was unable to fall in with his plans.

"I'm sorry, Richard, honestly—but my aunts are arriving; and I've got to meet them—I told you."

"Leave a note," said Richard lightly. "Back in half an hour."

"I can't. I'm meeting their train." And also, she added to

herself, seeing that they don't pay for their own taxi, and seeing that they have a decent dinner in the flat instead of wasting their money taking me out, *and* seeing that they sleep in the beds and let me sleep on the sofa, without arguing and—"

"D'you mean to say," enquired Richard, "that you're throwing me down for a couple of aunts?"

"They're rather special aunts—I'm awfully sorry, Richard."

"But this is a *party,*" said Richard. "Best frock and a night club."

"It sounds lovely, but I've known about this other thing for ages, and I can't let them come to—to just an empty flat and a note."

"Make it a convincing note. 'Called away—Urgent.' "

Rae laughed.

"It's easy—but I can't do it. Some other night, Richard."

"My God, you're serious!"

"Well—yes."

"What's the matter with these aunts? Totally incapacitated?"

"Well, no. It's just that I'm going off, and they're coming to—to—well, I mean, they're coming, and I must be there. You wouldn't—" She paused.

"Wouldn't what?"

"Well, if you didn't have anything else to do, I was going to say they're rather sweet, if you'd—if you'd like to—"

Men and Angels

"Darling," came Richard's incredulous voice, "you're not asking me to spend an evening with your *aunts*?"

"Not a whole evening—of course not."

"Not even the fraction of an evening. The suggestion," said Richard, "is appalling. It even has a sinister ring. Besides, I told you—this is a party."

"I forgot. But I can't come, Richard—I'm so sorry."

"You're adamant?"

"Well—yes."

"Pity. Enjoy the aunts," said Richard lightly, he was gone, and Rae put down the receiver with a slight feeling of sickness. What had she expected? she asked herself. A man on leave, fitting in all he could, making the most of his time—would he spend an evening sitting on the wobbly chair looking at Aunt Hester and Aunt Anne? Rae blushed hotly at her stupidity in suggesting it. She should have said 'No' and left it at that. She should have said a firmer and less regretful 'No' and rang off. Well, it was too late and perhaps the party would make him forget how naïve she had been.

She met Judy for lunch in town, chiefly to exchange last-minute reminders. Judy, in a new suit which she called her Artist-in-the-Country, ate a large and heavy-looking omelet and looked across at Rae.

"I didn't have time to clear those two drawers in my room for your aunts," she said penitently. "And I left two pairs of shoes and—"

"I'll get things straightened out," promised Rae. "I'll have a lot of time—I'm not meeting them until seven."

"Meeting them? I thought Richard had decided to have a party—he told me when I rang him up this morning. Haven't you heard from him?"

"Yes—he asked me, but I said I couldn't go."

"Couldn't—why?"

"Because I've told you—I've got to meet the—"

"But good lord," exclaimed Judy in astonishment, "you don't mean you couldn't have left a note or something?"

"I'm going to the station. I suppose I could have sent them a wire to say I wouldn't be there," acknowledged Rae, "but I—well, I didn't want to."

"Well, they're your aunts," said Judy, "but I can't see Richard being very pleased at being shovelled aside to make room for—"

"He wasn't very pleased," admitted Rae, "but you ought to understand, even if he didn't. They're coming up to London, which they loathe, and living in a flat, which they loathe even more, and for the next three weeks they'll rub and scrub and wear themselves out and—"

"I see all that," said Judy, "but the future, which is Richard, is more important than the past, which is your aunts. You should have gone out with him—you know they wouldn't have minded."

"They wouldn't, but I would. It's the first time I've spent

my holiday away from home, and I wanted to give them the whole of this week-end."

"Well, have it your own way," said Judy indifferently. "It all comes of having a sense of duty, which I'm glad I haven't. What a noisy place this is, Rae—d'you often come here?"

"Yes. It is rather noisy to-day—what's all that hooting?"

"All the traffic in London piled up outside this door, blowing their whistles, it sounds like. What's nicest, Rae— trifle or treacle tart?"

"Treacle tart."

"Then order two, and tell them to step on it—I ought to be getting off."

She attacked the tart with relish, glancing up as a policeman entered the door and stood looking about him. After pausing to speak to the occupants of the tables nearby, he made his way towards Rae and Judy.

"I heard him say there was a terrific traffic block," said Rae nervously as he approached. "Judy, where did you leave—"

"That your car, Miss?" enquired the policeman, his round, rosy young face shocked. "Blue two-seater, number—"

"It's mine," said Judy. "It can't be causing any jam—it's such a tiddly little car, and I put it right against the edge of the pavement, so you'll probably find that it's something else that's causing the—"

"Your car, Miss," said the policeman in slow, measured tunes, "is standing where—"

"Do I have to move it this minute? I'm just in the middle of treacle tart."

"The car," said the policeman, going back to the beginning, "has no business to be left in—"

"No—I'm terrible sorry. I was so *hungry,* and there isn't a garage nearer than—"

"The car," interrupted the policeman, "should have been parked in the—"

"I know—Court Street. But it was full! I asked the man to push it in, but he said it looked as though someone had done too much pushing already."

"The car," said the policeman, stiffened by the hideous discordancies of a hundred hooters, "the car must be—"

"Oh, all right—I'll take it away. Am I under arrest?"

"No," said the policeman regretfully.

"Oh! Well, then, good-bye, Rae." Judy moved to the door, issuing directions over her shoulder. "Don't forget— Monday at Sheafton-by-Thorpe. Don't get out at Thorpe it may sound the same, but it's not the right station."

"Sheafton-by-Thorpe," said Rae. "Good-bye."

"And remember about—"

"The car," droned the policeman, "is—"

"Oh yes, oh yes—why do they make all that *row*?" asked Judy impatiently.

"All those persons whom you have kept waiting," said the policeman, "have important business to—"

"Important? What's more important," demanded Judy, "than finishing off this treacle tart? 'Bye, Rae," she shouted from the door. "Sheafton-by-Thorpe, Monday."

Rae embarked upon the journey on Monday with a fund of recently acquired knowledge. Her aunts, making polite enquiries about Thorpe, had asked what county it was in, and Rae had been obliged to confess that she did not know.

"But you're going there!" said Aunt Hester. "Do you mean to tell me you don't even know what county you're going into?"

"I'm afraid not."

"Well, where is this place near?"

"Near?"

"What is its market town—county town?"

"County town?"

"It must be the echo," said Aunt Hester. "I don't know how you girls manage to live at all with so little knowledge of anything."

"Instinct, dear," said Aunt Anne.

"Well, I hope instinct will get her to Thorpe—what station are you going from, Rae?"

"Oh, Judy said Paddington—or was it Marylebone?"

"Either would do," commented Aunt Anne. "They've both got trains—you just get into one and say 'Thorpe'."

"Rae?"

"Yes, Aunt Hester?"

"Fetch me an atlas."

The atlas had been useless, but the aunts, burrowing, had unearthed an old map marked LONDON & WEST.

Shaking off the dust of a year, they found that Thorpe was not marked, but Sheafton-by-Thorpe appeared on the thinnest of branch lines in Buckinghamshire.

"Well, now we know where you're going," said Aunt Hester. "You go from Marylebone, and you change, obviously, at this place here—Pierstone. Then your stations are Pierstone, West Plumbley, Thorpe and Sheafton. Did Judy tell you that?"

"No."

"Well, see if I'm not right," concluded Aunt Hester.

She was quite right. Rae, enquiring at Pierstone, found that she had to change. Puffing out of the station in the shabby little train, its progress reminded her of the game she had played as a child with dandelion seeds. A strong puff, and half the seeds vanished. At West Plumbley, at least half of the scanty number of passengers disembarked. Another puff, and at Thorpe half the remainder got off and two of the three carriages were disconnected. Rae gathered her things together and was ready when the train slowed down again, but it was not her destination. She saw a sign reading:

SHEAFTON ABBOTT

HALT

Men and Angels

Rae was the last remaining passenger; the train was now running exclusively on her behalf. Looking out of the window as the train moved on again, she wondered where the Sheafton Abbotts were housed. So far as she could see, there was not a dwelling in sight. Trees, a lane, a little winding river, but no houses. Two cows in a field, but no sign of a farmhouse.

It was pretty, she thought, but a little too uninhabited for her taste. She had been brought up in the country, but her parents' house had stood at the end of a well-populated village. Shops were close at hand, transport facilities abounded. This—Rae glanced out at the tiny station coming into view—this was going a little too far.

She stepped out, the sole arrival. The engine-driver stepped down from the cab, passed her with a nod, and vanished into the shed which served as a station. Rae was alone.

She picked up her suitcase, walked to the end of the short platform and into the lane beyond. There was no sign of Judy, but Judy was not noted for punctuality. Rae dusted a square on the platform's edge, and seated herself.

It was seven minutes by her watch when she heard the approach of a car; she stood up, saw the familiar blue and waved. The car drew up, and Rae swung her suitcase into the back.

"Hello, Judy."

"Hello, Rae. Get in."

Rae got in, noting something subdued in the small figure next to hers. She glanced at Judy and saw that something was wrong. She wondered what it was, but knew she would not have to wonder long.

"How's everything?" she asked.

"Everything," said Judy slowly, "is hell, but don't ask me now, Rae, please. I don't know how I'm going to tell you."

Rae was silent, running over the possibilities. Richard? It was unlikely that anything had happened to him—Judy would have wired or telephoned. Something might have happened to her father or mother—no, not her father—he was dead already. There was an uncle, and a friend....

"Are your people all right?"

"Who? Oh, *them.* They're all right," said Judy, staring straight ahead.

"Is it the job?" asked Rae. "Too much temperament among the artists?"

"No."

"Then what? You'd better tell me, Judy—that is, if it's anything I've got to know eventually. What's bothering you?"

Judy edged the car to the side of the road and, bringing it to an abrupt stop, switched off the engine. They were in a wood, and the sun was making a lace pattern on the ground. A little stream went by with agitated whispers. The silence made Rae feel oppressed, and she turned to face her companion. To her horror, she saw one, two, and then an unceasing flow of tears coursing down Judy's face.

"Oh, Rae," she said, between a gulp and a sob, "I don't

know how to tell you!"

Rae had to steady herself for a moment. She had never seen Judy cry—Judy stormed when she was angry, and was sullen when she felt sad. Rae had seen tears of rage in her eyes, but they had never fallen.

"Don't cry, Judy darling," she urged gently. *"Talk."*

Judy gave a wail that made Rae realise that the tears were the result of a long period of pressure. With the wail came a fresh torrent, and Judy, feeling in vain for a handkerchief, groped in the cubby-hole of the car and brought out a square that might have once been a handkerchief but was now an oily rag.

"Wait a bit," said Rae.

She slipped out of the car, opened her suitcase, and extracted two of the most serviceable handkerchiefs she could find. With these, she returned to her seat.

"Here," she said.

Judy took them, wiped her eyes, blew her nose, and pushed the damp hair off her face.

"I'm a silly damn fool," she said shakily. "Crying's a lot of use, but I had to cry or burst. Or do murder. I knew I had a foul temper, but I've never wanted to kill anybody before."

"Who?" asked Rae.

"R-Richard. He—he isn't here."

"Isn't here?" repeated Rae, uncomprehending. "Then—"

"He hasn't come," said Judy. "He hasn't come, and he

isn't coming."

"I—I see," said Rae, quietly.

"You don't—you *don't* see," cried Judy. "You don't see anything. Oh, Rae, I hate him so much at this moment that if I heard that—"

"Don't be silly, Judy," broke in Rae. "You mean he—he changed his mind about—"

"Let me tell it to you, Rae. And then you can see why I——" Judy stopped and began in a steadier tone. "He was coming down on Saturday, as you know."

"Yes."

"Well, he didn't come. He rang Mother up and just said he wouldn't be down—just like that. No explanation. He said, 'Tell Judy not to be angry.' I turned up on Saturday, and Mother told me, and I tried to ring him up—I tried everywhere, but I couldn't get him. Well, I waited all Sunday—nothing. I tried him again on Sunday evening— nothing. His hotel just said 'Out, out, out'—Had he had my message? Oh yes, they'd given him all my messages—but he'd done nothing about them. Then Monday came—today, and I felt desperate. There you were, arriving—at his invitation, and he'd just—vanished. Mother thought nothing of it—we often say we're coming and then we don't, but this was different. I didn't tell her why it was important, but I went on worrying. Then I suddenly decided I'd go up and see what had happened."

"Go up to—"

Men and Angels

"To his hotel."

"How did you know he wasn't with—with me?"

"If he'd been with you," said Judy, "why would he have said I wasn't to be angry? He knew I'd be glad, and that I wouldn't have cared—in that case—whether he came or whether he stayed with you. It was that that worried me. Well, this morning I couldn't bear it any more, and so I drove up to Town and I found Richard at his hotel. He wasn't surprised at all—he said, 'Ah, I thought you'd be here,' and then I asked him what the hell he thought he was doing and—and he—he told me—"

"Well?"

There was a long pause, and Judy spoke in an unsteady voice.

"It's—it's Rosanna," she said.

"Rosanna?"

"Yes. Oh, I know what you're thinking, Rae—you're thinking that no man could look at Rosanna after looking at you. Well, they can. Men can do anything. Men can—"

"But he doesn't know her!"

"He met her. There was a party and—"

"On Friday?"

"Yes, on Friday. Richard gave a party to a crowd of his Kenya cronies, all here on leave, and they went to the Waterside, and there was Rosanna doing a turn. Richard remembered she'd been with us at Madame Soublin's, and he got her

61

over to his table and told her he was my brother—and I suppose they went on from there. She said she was having a party, and Richard promised to stay in Town for it. Since Friday, they've been tucked in each other's shirt-fronts. They were out for the day on Saturday and went back for the show. All day Sunday and, for all I know, all night too.... I'm sorry, Rae, but you can't really take a close look at Rosanna and imagine she'd stick to Madame Soublin's rules of behaviour, can you?"

"I've never taken a close look," said Rae.

"Well, I have. Rae, I wish I'd cut off my right ear—both my ears—before I got you into this. But how could I know that my own brother was just another man? How could I know that a Rose Lewis could get hold of him? If I'd known that he was going to the Waterside that night, I wouldn't even have worried—I wouldn't have imagined for a moment that he could look twice at her. I asked Richard what she'd done to attract him, but I couldn't get him to talk. And I suppose I didn't give him much chance—I was busy putting all my thoughts into words, and they were pretty ugly thoughts. Then he told me to go away, and I wouldn't, so he locked me in his bathroom and told the management to let me out. And I—I came back here to— to tell you."

There was a long silence. There was a good deal to think of, but Rae found it difficult to think at all. She sat for some time turning the same thought over and over, and then spoke quietly.

"Hadn't we better be going on?"

Men and Angels

"Do you want to go on?" asked Judy. "I mean, you'll have to stay tonight, but if you like, I won't go back to the school—I'll ring up and make an excuse, and then wait here till the morning and drive you back to the train."

"Can't I get a—"

"You can't get a bus, if that's what you're going to say. And there's no transport of any kind at home—but you don't have to stay down here, Rae. I mean, Mother and the other two know nothing about anything—they just think you're coming down for the air or something, but I got you into this and I'd like to stay and get you out."

Out where? wondered Rae. She would not go back to the flat; let the aunts have their pleasant little dreams about the imaginary young man. Where else could she go?

"If your mother doesn't mind," she began, "I'll stay."

"Mother? She won't know whether you're there or not. But what'll you *do,* Rae? You don't know what it's like here —and you've no car and—"

"Let's go on," said Rae. "You just drop me and go off, Judy—it's a lovely bit of country and I'll eat and grow fat and—"

"Not at my home you won't," prophesied Judy.

"Well, at least I'll eat—let's go."

Judy started the car and drove for another mile or two. A large iron gateway came into view, and Judy turned into it. She drove a few hundred yards, turned a corner, and Rae saw before them a large, square, ugly building.

"This is it," said Judy.

She seized the suitcase from Rae and led her up the wide steps to the front door. Throwing it open, she stepped into a shabby hall.

"Mummy!" she called.

There was no response.

"Probably in the kitchen," said Judy, putting the suitcase down. "Come on—we'll look."

She led Rae towards one of the doors opening off the hall and greeted a grey-haired woman coming towards them.

"Oh Miss Beckwith, where's Mummy? This is Rae."

"How do you do?" said Miss Beckwith, extending a hand. "Did you have a pleasant journey?"

"Yes thank you," said Rae.

"Your Mother's in the library, I think," went on Miss Beckwith.

"Oh—this way, Rae," said Judy.

She pushed open the door of the library, and a tall elderly man turned from one of the long windows.

"Hello Uncle Bertram. This is Rae. Rae, this is my—"

"How do you do?" said the General, extending a hand. "Did you have a pleasant journey?"

"Yes, thank you," said Rae.

"Your mother's upstairs, Judy," said the General. "I expect you'll find her in Rae's room."

"Come on, Rae."

They went up a flight of stairs and walked along a long corridor. Judy threw open the door of a room at the end.

"Oh, here you are, Mummy," she said. "Here's Rae."

A white-haired woman came towards them, a hand outstretched.

"How nice to see you, Rae," she said. "Did you have a—"

"Yes, Mother," said Judy. "She did."

Chapter Five

Later that evening, Rae stood in the hall to see Judy off.

"Good-bye," she said. "When will you be back?"

"Friday, I hope, but Saturday for sure, said Judy. "Look, Rae, if you can't stick it, ring me up and I'll come out."

"I shall be all right," said Rae.

"You don't *know,* Rae—you've never lived in this house. It was all very well when we were young and things were—were alive, but now—"

"Thanks for worrying," said Rae steadily, "but there's really nothing to worry about."

"Honest?"

"Honest."

"Bless you," said Judy unexpectedly, and was gone.

The front door closed, and Rae stood in the silent hall and let her misery close in on her. She was here for almost three weeks—twenty-one days. She was in this large, bare house with the woman with white hair and the woman with grey hair and the old man with the reddish whiskers. There was nothing to go out in, nothing to stay in for. She was here at Richard

Men and Angels

Ashton's invitation, and Richard was enjoying himself in London with Rosanna Lee.

At the thought of them together, Rae's misery almost overcame her. It was one thing to tell Judy she didn't care—it was quite another to hold her head up and behave, for the next three weeks, as though she found everything in this house that she had hoped to find. She looked desperately towards the stairs, seized by an irresistible impulse to rush up to her bedroom, pack her suitcase and make her escape.

A door behind her opened, and Rae, pulling herself together, turned to see Judy's mother coming towards her. She wondered how so plain a woman could have produced children as good-looking as Richard and Judy.

Lady Ashton was not a plain woman, but Rae was not a student of bone structure or skin texture. She saw merely the wrinkled cheeks, the white hair, the neat but uninteresting clothes.

"There you are, Rae my dear. Have you been seeing Judy off?"

"Yes."

"What a pity she couldn't stay, but we must try to look after you. Would you like me to show you the house, so that you can find your own way about?"

"Thank you."

They began a slow progress from room to room, and Rae did her best to appear interested. The house was not a showplace—the rooms were lofty and well-proportioned, but they were shabby and sparsely furnished. The two walked along corridors and looked into bedrooms with old-fashioned brass bedsteads; they walked in and out of unused sitting-rooms and playrooms; they skirted a landing which, Lady Ashton explained, led to the General's suite. They inspected a vast bathroom—"It's the only one in the house," Lady Ashton explained regretfully. Rae, staring wide-eyed at the huge boarded-in bath and the geyser evidently of Heath Robinson design—decided that it was the only one of its kind anywhere.

"There's far too much room for us now, of course," said Lady Ashton, "but it was a very good house in which to bring up children, and that's why I came here. All four children were brought up here—they were born abroad, you know, but I came home with them when they were very young. There was plenty of growing room, both in the house and in the garden."

The placid voice went on, and Rae made a polite pretence of listening. She was deeply relieved when Lady Ashton at length opened a door and ushered her in.

"I'm going to leave you here," she said. "This is the drawing-room—you can see that the children weren't allowed in here—it has scarcely any battle scars. Sit down, my dear, and rest after your journey. If you would like a book, you'll find a good many on that bookshelf, or on the little one near that window. I have to leave you to see to the dinner, because I do all the cooking myself."

"Can't I help?" offered Rae, anxious to escape being left

in the drawing-room with a book.

Lady Ashton smiled.

"That's very kind of you," she said, "but I really find it better to manage alone—I've done it for nearly five years, and I'm quite in a little rut, so I go on quietly. We have dinner at eight, and the General likes to change. You'll hear a gong at a quarter-past seven and another at five minutes to eight, and the General likes us to be punctual—now, is there anything you'd like? You'd like a peep at the garden before dinner, I expect; when you've rested a little, you can get through that door on to the terrace and look round."

"Thank you. Can't I—couldn't I lay the table or something?" asked Rae desperately.

"How kind of you—Judy never offers to do anything, the lazy little thing," returned the sweet, soft voice. "But you see, we're very fortunate—the gardener's daughter makes herself useful, and Miss Beckwith helps a great deal, so there's really nothing you can do. Now, are you sure you'll be comfortable?"

"Yes, thank you," said Rae.

Yes, she would be comfortable, she mused, sitting on the arm of a chair and staring out at an expanse of moss-covered paving which was no doubt the terrace. Comfortable, bored, trapped. Judy's mother was sweet, but if she had to listen to that well-bred monotone for three weeks, she'd...

The door opened and Rae, turning, saw Miss Beckwith coming in with some flowers.

"Oh, there you are, my dear," she said. "You've been seeing Judy off, I expect."

"Yes."

"We miss her when she goes—she's such a lively little thing that she stirs us all up. Would you like to see the house, and then you'll be able to find your own way about?"

"Well, no—thank you. Lady Ashton took me round."

"Oh, good. It's a pity there's only the one bathroom, but we manage very well on the whole. The General likes to have it to himself in the mornings at half-past seven, but he's very punctual, and he goes in exactly at half-past and he's out by ten minutes to eight, so we arrange our baths before or after, as we please. I expect you like getting up early and getting a little breather before breakfast?"

"Oh no—I mean, yes. Well, sometimes I—"

"You'll have to see how you feel," said Miss Beckwith in her quiet, kind way. "I expect you'll be glad of a rest after your journey."

"No—yes. I mean, it wasn't really very far—the journey. I mean."

"No, not far, but train journeys are so full of bustle and confusion, don't you find? And so dirty. Of course, I'm forgetting how young you are—you can probably take these things in your stride, as it were—has Lady Ashton told you about meals?"

"Dinner at eight, she said."

Men and Angels

"Yes, and the General likes to change. We have breakfast at eight, but we don't come down—I get the trays ready overnight, and the gardener's daughter makes the toast and leaves our trays outside our rooms. Sometimes, of course, people prefer a very large breakfast, and so Lady Ashton comes down to prepare it. Do you take a large one, or just an ordinary one?"

Thus cornered, Rae said that she took an ordinary one.

"In that case, you'll find your tray outside at eight o'clock," proceeded Miss Beckwith. "Lunch is at one, but I expect you'll want to take sandwiches and go for nice long tramps. If you'll just let me know when you come down in the morning, I'll tell the gardener's daughter and she'll prepare you a nice little packet. Do you care for fish paste?"

"Yes, thank you," said Rae automatically.

"I must tell her. Tea in here at four, if you're back by then, and remember, if you come back hungry, you mustn't hesitate—you must ask for a boiled egg."

"Thank you."

"And now I think I must leave you and go upstairs to change—I always go up about this time, and then I can be out of the bathroom before the General comes up—if you want a book, you'll find—"

"Oh yes, thank you—Lady Ashton showed me."

"I don't know whether you care for sea stories," said Miss Beckwith. "I'm just reading one—here it is—it's called *Under the Deep*. It was written by a charming man who went down, unfortunately, on the *Helena*. We all knew him very well—-it was quite sad. Do read his book if you care to —I'll leave it for you."

The door closed; Rae sank on to the sofa and stared straight before her. Miss Beckwith's soft footfall died away; there was nothing to be heard except the twitter of birds. Rae looked round wildly for a wireless and relapsed into hopelessness. None. Could people live nowadays, she wondered desperately, without a wireless? There must—there *must* be one. Judy wouldn't sit here, shut away in a huge tomb, with nothing but birds and books—she would open the door and shout loudly until somebody came and supplied her with what she wanted. But she was the daughter of the house—and she was Judy.

The minutes passed slowly. Rae got up and walked to the door through which she could reach the terrace; a wave of utter desolation engulfed her, and she leaned her forehead against the pane, making no attempt to fight her way back to common sense. She knew fairly well now the kind of household in which she was fixed; there was peace, order, even a certain faded elegance, there was kindness and a desire for her comfort. But she was as far removed from these people, from their way of life, as a—as a—she struggled to find something that approximated to her own situation, and could think of nothing better than a fox descending suddenly upon a nest of broody hens. She raised her head, and a stiffening thought pierced her gloom. She was not the fox. The fox was Richard Ashton, who had got her down here under false—the most false, the most black of pretences, and left her marooned while he—Rae drew a breath of pure rage—while he danced round Rosanna Lee. He was taking her to the same places, using the same words, kissing her with the same smooth, lying lips. He could be under no illusions about his family and the life they led; he had asked her down here expressly to relieve him of the loneliness and the boredom which were now crushing her.

Rae's nature was calm; she was roused much more easily in laughter than to wrath, but she could be angry. Her temper rose slowly, but it rose high, and it was high now. She longed to have Richard before her; ordinarily slow of speech, she now had the words, the fluency to tell him, with scorching effect, what she thought of him. The picture of Richard standing before her, stripped of his glibness and poise, made her feel better than she had done since she had heard Judy's news.

She stared out, unseeing. A discreet little gong sounded, but she heard nothing. She was only recalled to the present by the opening of the door and the entrance of General Fitzroy.

"Ah," he said, "you're here. I expect Judy went off all right?"

"Yes, she did."

Conversation here, she reflected, was somewhat repetitive. An original and two copies. She waited patiently—he would scarcely offer to show her round the house, but he would undoubtedly point out the garden and the bookshelf. She looked up at him, and thought suddenly of the Duke of Wellington, without knowing why, and without knowing that everybody, on meeting the General, always thought of the Duke of Wellington.

General Fitzroy was, in fact, the popular conception of the Iron Duke. The commanding presence, the erect bearing, the jutting crag of nose, the eagle glance—these made the stranger think automatically of the most prominent figure emerging from the forgotten pages of their history books. In evening dress, with his shirt front gleaming, the General made an impressive figure, and a pair of bushy whiskers with a distinct reddish tinge added the last picturesque touch.

"I expect," he said, "you've been looking round the garden."

"Well, no," said Rae. "I stayed in here."

The General looked surprised.

"I thought you must have gone out," he said. "It's difficult to hear the dressing gong if one's outside."

"Dr-dressing gong? You mean it went?" asked Rae, panic beginning to creep over her once more.

The General pulled a watch out of his waistcoat pocket.

"Seven thirty-seven," he announced. "It went—let me I see—twenty-two minutes ago."

"Oh!" Rae gave a gasp. "I'm terribly sorry—I must have missed it. I'll go—I mean, I'll rush like anything."

The General opened the door for her and, glancing at the watch he held, made a further calculation.

Men and Angels

"You have just under twenty-eight minutes," he said. "It doesn't give you very long."

"No," said Rae, earnestly. "But I'll rush and—I'll really be down."

She went through the doorway with as much dignity as possible and, once outside, sped up the stairs and galloped down the corridor. She reached her room, threw open her suitcase, and scattered its contents at random. Why hadn't Judy warned her? She had brought suits, woollen dresses, but nothing remotely resembling an evening dress. That sort of thing—did people still? Breathless, Rae shook out a silk dress—the only one she had with her—and changed rapidly. She flew to the dressing-table, scampered back to get her brush and comb, stood before the old-fashioned table and swiftly did her hair. Throwing down the comb, she hurried out of the room and was half-way along the corridor when she drew herself up with a jerk and looked at her watch.

Four minutes! She had been exactly four minutes. Turning, she crept cautiously back to her room and shut herself in. She couldn't go down yet. They'd expect her to have a bath after the dirty train journey. They'd think she'd just thrown her clothes on instead of dressing with leisurely care. She would get down in time, but only just in time.

Walking to one of the two large windows, she stood looking out at what seemed to her a desolate world. There was not a house, not a human in sight. She might just as well, she thought dismally, be in the middle of a prairie. Her ideas on prairies were vague, but she felt that they were vast expanses whose inhabitants experienced none of the cosy neighbourliness which was to be enjoyed in London. Tomorrow she would be sent out to wander with her fish paste among the pathless woods and the winding roads, to come in to a boiled egg and a book. It was not an exhilarating prospect. One day, prayed Rae, let me get even with Richard Ashton for doing this to me.

She found that the thought of Richard could still hurt, and was depressed to learn that his personality had a stronger effect on her than his character. Even more depressing was the realisation that she had not only fallen in love unasked, but had chosen a thoroughly unworthy object.

Six minutes to.... She could go down now. Rae made her second sortie into the corridor, and walked firmly down the stairs and into the drawing-room. The General took out his watch and beamed at her in congratulation.

"Ah-ha!" he said. "You just did it."

As he spoke, Lady Ashton and Miss Beckwith came in, and the gong—sounded, presumed Rae, by the gardener's daughter—gave its subdued summons. Rae, her eyes widening, saw the two ladies walking slowly towards the dining-room and the General, with the slightest of bows, offering her his arm. In a dream, she took it, and found herself following Lady Ashton's grey lace and Miss Beckwith's black-with-sequins.

The dining-room was as large as the drawing-room; the shrunken table, its last leaf shed, occupied a small space in the middle of the polished floor. Lady Ashton seated herself at the head of the table and motioned Rae to a place beside her; Miss Beckwith went to a sideboard and served the soup, and the General brought the plates round.

Soup over, Miss Beckwith took the plates one by one to the sideboard and resumed her seat. The General rose, put down his napkin and raised the silver cover from a dish.

"Now let me see," he said. "Fish cutlets. These look very nice, Dorothy." Lady Ashton looked pleased at the compliment, and the General turned to Rae. "May I give you one?" he enquired.

"Thank you," said Rae, half rising from her seat. "Can't I come and—"

"No, no, no—sit down," urged the General. "There. Now"—he carried over two dishes and placed them before her—"will you help yourself to potatoes and peas?—Are these the last of the peas, Dorothy?"

"I'm afraid so," said Lady Ashton. "Blanche picked them—she can tell you better. What do you think, Blanche?" Miss Beckwith thought that there might be enough for another dish in a day or two. Rae took some of the last-dish-but-one and passed them to Lady Ashton.

"Thank you. Salt and pepper?"

"Thank you. Won't you—"

"Oh, thank you."

The fish was removed, plate by plate, by Miss Beckwith, who then placed a small custard glass before each person. Rae, examining hers, found it to be composed of strawberries and cream.

"This looks very nice," she said. "Are they your own?"

"Yes. But I've not been getting nearly so many strawberries this year," complained the General. "I hoped for a heavy crop, but in some way there hasn't been half the amount I expected. The gardener thinks it might be the dry weather. I suppose you can't grow much in London?"

"Bertram dear, they're in a flat," protested Lady Ashton.

"Yes, yes, of course! I'm always meaning to go up and take a look at you two girls, but I don't get the time. Used to go up regularly three times a week, but I can't do it more than once now. And nowadays I don't get much beyond my Club. You and Judy must come and have lunch with me one day."

"Thank you—we'd love to."

The General rose, took a decanter of port from the sideboard and placed it on the table before him. Rae tried nervously to remember whether port went round, and if so, which way, but it soon became clear that this port, at any rate, was staying where it was. Neither Lady Ashton nor Miss Beckwith drank it, and the General had no intention of throwing away his '97 on a girl of twenty.

A murmur from Lady Ashton informed Rae that the ladies were leaving. The General rose and opened the door and closed it behind them. Rae walked between Lady Ashton and Miss Beckwith to the drawing-room.

The evening which followed was the longest and the most agonising she had ever spent. There was, in the unending desert of stillness, one little oasis of movement—when the General came in and handed round coffee from the tray left ready on a table. For the rest, the party became four isolated and widely separated units. The General, on a high-backed chair near the window, read the *Spectator*. Lady Ashton looked through a pile of cookery books and made notes on a little pad. Miss Beckwith, at a table in a far corner, spread out her fortune-telling cards and began studying them with absorbed attention. Rae, picking a book at random, sat on the sofa and sank into a coma of despair.

The minutes ticked slowly by; Rae's watch told her it was five minutes since they had finished coffee, her stiff neck and aching back cried out that it was four times as long. The stillness was terrifying—she started at the rustle of the General turning a page, and leapt when Miss Beckwith shuffled the pack. Clearing her throat once, she thought sounded like a crack of thunder.

A gentle sound was heard at the door, and the General, rising, opened it, and admitted a splendid Golden Retriever. The beautiful animal came into the room and Rae, in an access of hope, put out a hand and made a coaxing sound. But the General resumed his seat, the dog sank down quietly beside him, and the interlude was over; silence fell like a heavy curtain. Rae, pretending to read, could hear the beating of her heart.

O God, she prayed, with more earnestness than she had used since her childhood, *O God, please get me out of this. They're all quite nice, O God, but please get me away where I can move and make a noise.*

After what seemed hours, there was a decided stir. Rae, looking up hopefully, saw the General look at his watch, fold his paper and rise.

"Five to nine, m'dear," he said to his sister. "Good night."

"Good night, Bertram."

"Good night, Blanche. Good night, my dear. I hope you'll sleep well after your journey."

"Thank you very much. Good night."

With his going, there was, if not a release of tension, an indefinable easing. Miss Beckwith put away her cards; Lady Ashton laid aside her books, and looked at Rae.

"I expect," she said kindly, "you'll want to go to bed."

Rae rose thankfully.

"Yes," she said. "I think I'll go up."

"If you want to listen to the wireless at any time," said Lady Ashton, "you can always go into the General's study and put it on. He always has the news on at nine, and if there's anything special, we go in and listen. I expect you listen a good deal, don't you?"

Rae was not sure how much she listened, but she had not until now experienced the horror of having nothing to listen to. Saying good night, she went upstairs, where she found that the gardener's daughter had tidied the things left scattered about the room, and turned down her bedclothes.

Rae undressed and, lying on the large, uncomfortable bed, made a solemn vow. She would get out of this, and soon. How, she didn't know—there was nobody she could ask to send her an urgent telegram. But she would wait until one of her aunts wrote to her—she would open the letter at the breakfast table—no—there was no breakfast table—she would open the letter at lunch—no—she would be out with the fish paste. She would open the letter at tea —that was it. She would open it with the boiled egg—she would open it and give a murmur of distress. From then on it would be easy.

Oh, dear!

Lady A.: What is it, my dear? Bad news, I expect.

My aunt—one of my aunts—she—*(overcome)*.

Lady A.: Dear me—you'll want to get home at once, I expect?

If you wouldn't mind—yes.

Lady A.: You shall go at once, my dear. Just finish up your egg and I'll order the taxi (wagon, buggy, cart, trap).

Trap. Yes, it was surely a trap. But when the letter came, she would be free....

Practising murmurs of distress, Rae fell asleep.

Chapter Six

The Fitzroys had owned, for two hundred years, a manor-house in Kent, and Bertram and his sister had lived in it until Dorothy was thirty-six when, to her brother's surprise and disgust, she married and went to live abroad. Bertram's life underwent no great change: he had a competent housekeeper and she engaged competent servants. Even when catastrophic changes had robbed his neighbours of their comforts, Bertram, returning from his various periods of military service, could still lie in bed until his shaving water arrived.

His housekeeper left, and Bertram never succeeded in replacing her. For the first time in his life, he engaged his own cook and parlour-maid—a distasteful proceeding which he seemed doomed to repeat every two months. The old type of servant gave place to the new; attics were replaced by bed-sitting-rooms; one free evening a week expanded to several free hours every day. Uncomplaining service was succeeded by unceasing demands, and the General's last stand against the march of progress took place on the morning he interviewed a pretty little brunette.

"O' course, I must have a wireless in my room," she stated.

The General told her, bluntly, that she could have four in her room, provided he could not hear them.

"But you've got to get it," said the maiden. "My last place had two."

"Really?"

"And I'd have to have an easy-chair, o' course, and a couple o' rugs in that sitting-room—it isn't what you might call cosy, is it? And my last place had every second weekend off, and—"

The General advised her to go back to her last place as soon as possible, and put his house up for sale.

His sister, now widowed and with four children, was back in England. She had bought a house in Buckinghamshire, in a district that would have suited the General very well, but he had no intention of accepting her invitation to make a home with her until her children were of an age to understand what was due to their uncle. When Judy, the youngest, was sixteen, the General left the Club at which he had resided for so long and joined the family at Thorpe.

His sister welcomed him warmly. She had living with her lifelong friend Miss Beckwith, a spinster of ample means, who had let her own house at Bexhill for six months in order to come and help Lady Ashton with the children. The six months were now six years, and Miss Beckwith had become a permanent member of the household. She, like Lady Ashton, was glad of Bertram's coming; a man, she said, made a great difference in a house.

The General certainly made a difference. Lady Ashton found at once that the light meals which had sufficed for herself and Blanche were regarded by her brother as mere preludes, well-got-up little appetisers. When this little misunderstanding was cleared up, the General went back for a time to his Club in London, and Lady Ashton bought a supply of cookery books and retired to her kitchen. She had no hope of getting a cook; the modern servant found Thorpe Lodge too far removed from the three paramount needs: buses, shops and cinemas. The last indoor servant had long since departed; only one gardener remained. Lady Ashton, who had looked upon cooking as a matter of doing up an egg or two, found herself making adventurous excursions into the mysteries of steaming and roasting. Zeal on the General's behalf became interest on her own; interest deepened into absorption, and Lady Ashton's happiest hours came to be spent in her kitchen. She learned, in time, to cook Bertram's favourite dishes to perfection; Blanche looked after his linen and laundry; he was not to be blamed when he came in time to regard the establishment as his own.

The three fell into a quiet, contented way of life, and the world passed them by. None of them missed it. The General kept his eye on the government of the country and told the ladies how it should be conducted; he considered that England's affairs were deteriorating, and dated their worsening from the time of his own and his contemporaries' withdrawal from public life. He looked from time to time to see what foreign countries were doing, and explained its sinister import over the dinner-table.

None of them had ever cared for music or the arts; the General, giving in to pressure by enthusiasts, had attended one or two operas; he had given his reasoned conclusion that it was one thing to write an opera and quite another to sit through it. Lady Ashton's sole recollection of educational walks round the world's galleries was that they were cool and quiet. Miss Beckwith had been for many years the unmusical companion of an indefatigably musical mother, and her past was an unhappy medley of symphonies and concertos, recitals and festivals, with the drawing-room given up to a string quartet. She and Lady Ashton, coming late in life to the problems of housework, dealt with them sensibly and competently, and to the gradual exclusion of every other interest. A bed, neatly made, smooth and tight, with hospital corners, gave Miss Beckwith more pleasure than chamber music had ever done; Lady Ashton's greatest ambition was now to get Bertram's curries exactly as he liked them. If either woman had a social conscience, she was too busy to hear it. They were both convinced that they took an intelligent interest in the affairs of the nation, but their sole contribution to its welfare was the recording of a Conservative vote at the appropriate times; it was not much, Blanche pointed out, but if everybody would do the same, there would be no cause for anxiety.

It was a placid, even a happy household, and its three inmates would have been astonished to learn that Rae found anything lacking.

Rae woke early on her first morning at Thorpe, and lay for a time listening to the birds. She had heard birds singing before, but she had never been in a place in which the singers had been up against so little competition. There were no steps to be heard, no voices indoors, no murmuring without; the house lay basking in the same peace—or sighing with the same tedium—as on the previous evening.

A soft shuffling told Rae that her breakfast had arrived; she acknowledged the soft knock and presently slipped out of bed and went into the passage and brought in her tray. There was a jug of coffee, a jug of hot milk, sugar, toast, butter and marmalade. Rae climbed into bed again, propped the tray up on her knees, and ate a light but satisfying breakfast.

Breakfast over, she lay staring at the bleak day ahead. She would like a bath; her watch told her that the General would be out of the bathroom, and she put on a dressing-gown and made her way down the long corridor and up the three stairs to the bathroom. The sound of water running, however, informed her that Lady Ashton or Miss Beckwith was inside; Rae made the long journey back to her bedroom.

She tried twice more, unsuccessfully, before getting in. Her bath over, she dressed, put her tray outside, and went slowly downstairs. The house seemed empty and, after looking into one or two rooms, she went upstairs again and began to tidy her room. She was interrupted by the sound of a knock, and found Miss Beckwith at her door.

"Good morning—did you sleep well?"

"Yes, thank you. I was just going to—"

"You won't make your bed, will you?" asked Miss Beckwith gently. "The gardener's daughter does all the rooms with me, and we have a nice little routine—I suppose you find in the flat that you can get through so much more if you have some kind of routine?"

Rae smiled, and forbore to mention that she and Judy had a routine by which they got through nothing whatever. "But you must let me do *something!*" she protested.

"No—this is your holiday, remember," said Miss Beckwith, giving her hand a little pat. "You must get all the fun you can, and forget about work. I wish there was a lake here for you to sail on—what a pity the sea isn't nearer. One of my uncles used to take me sailing when I was about your age, at Geneva. He went down later in the *Black Prince*— it was very sad."

Rae made a murmur of distress, and Miss Beckwith gave her another pat, this time of comfort.

"Never mind. Now you must run downstairs and go out and enjoy yourself."

Rae went downstairs once more and met Lady Ashton carrying a small packet.

"Oh, good morning, my dear. Did you sleep well?"

"Yes, thank you."

"I've had some sandwiches made for you—they're fish paste. Miss Beckwith told me you were very fond of fish paste. Do you think you'll be thirsty? I could put you up a little bottle of lemonade."

"No, thank you—it's very kind of you."

"I have a map somewhere," said Lady Ashton. "If only I could—Oh, there you are, Bertram."

"Good morning," said the General. "Did you sleep well?"

"Yes, thank you," said Rae.

"Good morning, Dorothy. A lovely morning."

"Isn't it? Bertram, where would that map be—the one that makes everything so clear? It would help Rae to find her way about."

"It's in the library," said the General. "Come along, my dear, and I'll get it for you."

The map found, he spread it on a table and ran a horny forefinger over it. Rae bent over it, and tried to look interested.

"Now if you start from *here,*" said the General, "you can make your way up that hill and walk along that ridge for a couple of miles—then you can drop down at that point there, or you can go and take this fork—it's rather difficult to see, but it's marked all right. There—you see it? Now, from there you can either go straight on to that little bend there, or you can—yes, I think this would be the better way—branch right and follow the stream. You'll pass a nice little bit of water

Men and Angels

just there—the children used to swim in it, but I've closed it for the past few years—you can't have people using it as a sort of lido. There now"—he folded the map and handed it to her—"I think you'll be able to find your way home safely. You can't get lost, whatever you do—come here and I'll show you why." He took a shallow bowl from the mantelpiece and held it before her. "Now this bowl," he said, "is pretty well an exact picture of the Thorpe country. Down at the bottom of the bowl is the village, Thorpe Bottom—it is, actually, just what it sounds —the bottom of this bowl made by the surrounding hills. You see?"

"Yes."

"Now up here is where we stand—not quite on the rim, but almost. You could keep on this level and walk completely round without catching a glimpse of Thorpe Bottom, and from Thorpe Bottom you can see nothing on the hills— that's what makes this part of the country so nice and quiet —we've all got our little dips or hummocks or woods to keep us to ourselves. I suppose you've noticed that?"

"Yes, I have."

"Good. You've got eyes in your head—not like Judy, who never notices anything beyond her nose. Now off you go and enjoy yourself. Why don't you take Bess with you?—The exercise will do her good."

Rae left the house, and, followed by Bess, walked through the garden and out at a gate leading into a wood. She had only one object—to get out of sight of the house, hide behind the nearest dip or hummock, and stay there until it was time to go back and ask for a boiled egg. The day had to be spent, but she was not going to spend it in walking, a pastime which she regarded as the slowest known, only second, in her estimation, to watching cricket. Bess appeared to share her views, and seemed ready to turn and go home at the first possible moment.

Rae wandered on listlessly, stopping now and again to survey the inanimate scene. Climbing on to a gate, she sat moodily on it, her thoughts gloomy. Less than thirty miles away was London, teeming with life, swift, supercharged.

She would have given all she had to be in the flat with her aunts, even if it meant tying a cotton duster round her head and going into the corners. Had they, she wondered, discovered that accumulation behind the gas-stove? Where was Judy? Would she ask the artist—whatever his name was— to paint her mother? How many hours were there between now and the week-end?

Rae, musing unhappily, became aware of unfamiliar sounds. She listened and heard them again: voices.

She waited; there was, after all, life on the planet. Yes—here it was; young life. Boys, two, in age about twelve. Rae wished wistfully that they were both ten years older.

The boys, pulling a little handcart between them, drew abreast of Rae, and looked at her with frank curiosity. She saw that they were brothers—they looked almost exactly alike, with brown freckled faces, clear grey eyes and thin, brown bare legs. They had passed her and were going on steadily when it occurred to Rae that they might prove to be the only humans she would see in the long day stretching ahead. She jumped off the gate and called after them impulsively.

"Hey!"

The boys turned swiftly, and Rae thought there was apprehension on their faces, but that was absurd—what was there to be apprehensive about? She walked up to them.

"Do you live here?" she asked.

The older boy nodded.

"Yes—Thorpe Farm, just over there."

"Just over where?" enquired Rae. "I haven't seen any human habitation since I came here yesterday. I was beginning to think I was in Siberia, only warmer."

"But you can see the farm, practic'ly," said the younger boy. "If you climb that tree, you can see it from the top branches, easily."

"Thanks—some other time," said Rae. "I'm staying at Thorpe Lodge."

Once again she thought she saw wariness in their eyes, but the next moment the older boy smiled.

"My name's Hugh and this is my young brother—his name's Alan. What's yours?"

"Rae Mansfield. Aren't you supposed to be at school?"

"We went at the beginning of the term," said Hugh, "but we were sent home. Fire."

"Fire! Did it do much damage?" asked Rae.

"Not 'smuch as it could have done," said Alan regretfully. "It burnt our dorm, though, and—"

"—and at first they put us into other dorms, but there weren't enough beds and it was overcrowding, so the school's been sent home for a fortnight till they get new beds and everything and get it all right again."

"Bad luck—for the school, I mean. Are you going anywhere in particular," asked Rae, "or can I come, too? I'm not really used to being alone in Siberia—I live in London."

"We used to live in London—at least, Croydon—that's just outside. We're just going down to the village—it's Tuesday."

"That's market day," explained Alan, seeing her bewilderment. "D'you want to see market day? It isn't much—just a few stalls, that's all."

"I'd like to come, if you don't mind."

The three walked on, Rae happy, the boys at ease.

"How long have you lived here?" she asked.

" 'Bout two years," said Hugh. "Before that we were in Croydon."

"You *said* that, silly," put in his brother. "That's twice you've said we were in Croydon."

"I didn't. The first time I said we *came* from there, and then I said we were there before. We came with my mother," he explained, "and she died just after we came, and now

Men and Angels

we live with my stepfather. His name's Selwyn— we call him Uncle Lewis, 'cos that's his name—Lewis Selwyn, but our name's Moore."

"Do you like being here?"

"Yes, a lot. I liked farms before—I mean, before we came to this one, but this is a jolly nice farm, nicer than the ones we used to stay on for hols before we came here. We've got cows and two horses, and pigs and a ferret, and Alan's got four white rabbits. He was going to sell one to-day, but there were rather a lot of strawberries so we didn't bring the rabbit—how long're you here for?"

"Three weeks, I'm afraid."

"Well, you can come and see the farm," said Hugh. "Uncle Lewis'd like to show it to you. He likes it like anything—he was in London, all his life until three years ago, working in an office."

"A Government office," said Alan.

"Yes. And then his grandmother left him some money and—"

"His godmother, silly."

"Well, his godmother. He didn't know anything about it —that she was going to leave it to him, and he says it knocked him sideways."

"Endways."

"*Side*ways. He didn't know what to do, and he went on working just as though he'd got no money, and one day he had to come down here to see somebody, and he saw the farm and from that minute he wanted it. But you can't buy a farm straight away—you have to wait ages, but he got it in the end. Uncle Lewis tries to learn farming, but he never will—he doesn't even look like a farmer, Mart says."

"Mart?"

"Martha—she's our housekeeper. She's nice. She and her cousin do all the work."

"Her cousin's potty," put in Alan nonchalantly, "but she's nice, too. Her name's Reeny."

They came out on to a wider road and, for the first time, Rae caught sight of the village lying below them. The road descended in a series of bends; the little cart was disposed to go more swiftly now, and Hugh put it in front, where it pulled him along like a puppy straining at the lead.

The village consisted of little more than two rows of whitewashed cottages. The market stalls were placed on the roadside beyond the farthest cottage, but the boys made no attempt to approach them. Instead, Rae found that they were to do a house-to-house sale. The sales organisation looked fairly efficient—the door being opened, Hugh uttered the one word 'Strawberries'; Alan did the weighing on a toy-like machine and Hugh collected the money. Before the last of the fruit disappeared, Rae had a thought.

Look, she said. "I'll buy those. Our strawberries aren't doing so well this year, I'm told. I'll pay you for them and take them home with me."

Men and Angels

"Home to the Lodge?" enquired Hugh slowly.

"Well yes, of course—I'm not going back to London for three weeks."

The boys appeared curiously hesitant, and Rae, a little puzzled, added: "Of course, if you've promised them to someone, then—"

"No, they aren't promised," said Hugh.

"Well, let me buy them, then."

The two boys looked at one another.

"Go on," said Alan. "Let her have 'em."

"All right," said Hugh. "You can buy them, but just say you bought 'em in the market, see? Because you did, in a way."

Rae gave them a long look.

"See here," she said in her cool, slow way. "No funny business?"

Two pairs of the most innocent eyes she had ever looked into were raised to hers.

"*What* funny business?" asked Alan.

"*I'm* asking *you*. Whose strawberries are they?"

"Ours."

"Off your own place?"

"Some."

"And the others?"

There was a pause. Rae saw that both chins were set in an obstinate line.

"Just a minute," she said slowly. "I'm not here to clean the place up or anything. I'm just staying with—with friends, and they did happen to mention that the strawberries—what I mean is, I wouldn't like to spend my hard-earned money on something that I could go out and pick in their garden as easily as—as you appear to have done."

"We didn't go into their garden," said Hugh.

"But these *are* their strawberries."

"Some. But we bought them. Honestly, we bought them."

"Honestly—strictly honestly, you couldn't have done," said Rae.

"We aren't doing anything," said Hugh; "but if we tell you, you'll go back there and—"

"—and you'll poke your nose in," said Alan in sudden indignation. "We've sold things every hols, and nobody's worried, and now you come and—"

"I'm *staying* with them," explained Rae patiently. "If I were staying with you, you wouldn't—well, you wouldn't like me to do anything—peculiar, would you?"

"'Course not. And we're not doing anything peculiar, either. What we're doing, we're just sort of—of trading. We buy something and then we sell it."

"That's all right. But how do you *get* it?"

There was a very long pause, but Rae was content to wait. Something, she saw, was emerging.

"Well, *their* gardener," said Hugh slowly at last, "is keen

Men and Angels

on Mart."

"Mart? Oh yes—Mart. And so?"

"And so when he saw us taking our stuff to the market for pocket-money in the hols, he said he had a right to let us have stuff out of his garden that was sort of extra—that the people didn't need, and that would only get wasted. So he said, 'Call on your way down on Tuesdays and see me'—and so we do. And we pay him straight away—"

"—and we don't go in at all," said Alan. "We stand at the garden gate and we don't even look inside."

They stood silent, looking up at Rae.

"Are you going to tell them?" enquired Hugh after a time.

"No," said Rae. "I'm not. If you don't mind, I won't buy the strawberries, but I told you—I didn't come down here to clean up the place. People can look after their own gardens—and gardeners."

"That's all right," said Alan, brushing the whole matter aside. "Let's sell this last lot."

The last lot sold, the three turned to do the slow journey up the hill. Rae, looking at her watch, saw that it was almost noon.

"You going home?" asked Hugh.

"No. I'm going to find a nice picnic spot and eat my lunch."

"All by yourself?" asked Alan in surprise.

"All by myself—why not?"

"Well, it doesn't sound much fun. Why don't you come home and eat with us? We've got lots."

Rae hesitated. She found the boys good company and was not anxious to return to her lonely state, but she could scarcely she felt, walk into a stranger's house with no more solid backing than an invitation from his schoolboy sons.

"Tell you what," urged Hugh. "You come back with us and see Mart, and if you want to stay *then,* then stay. Come on."

Ray came on. A farm, she reflected, was an open place; if there was a welcome, she would stay—if not, she could make a graceful exit.

They walked steadily up the hill, the cart now trailing behind. They passed no traffic of any kind, and the road was as deserted as when they had made the descent. At a curve about half-way up, the boys stopped and pointed.

"Look," said Alan. "If you sort of look through the trees up there, you'll see a roof—not our house roof, but the cowhouse roof. See?"

Rae peered.

"Well, yes, I think—"

Nobody ever knew what she thought. There was a curious sound on the road somewhere above them—a whirring and a rustle. Before Rae had time to swing round to see what was coming, Hugh and Alan had dived for the hedge, pulling the cart after them. Hugh, with a belated remembrance of Rae,

Men and Angels

turned with an outstretched hand, but he was too late. Round the bend came a vehicle which Rae, in the second before it hit her, identified as a bath chair. The next moment it caught her shoulder, swung her into the hedge and went bowling on down the hill. Rae, sitting on the bush against which she had been thrown, had a glimpse of a red, angry face surmounted by a hat of the kind worn by polo players.

"Silly gel," screamed a voice.

The bath chair vanished round the bend below. Rae sat still, stupefied. Hugh and Alan were extricating themselves from the hedge opposite; the cart lay on its side near them.

"Oh, golly, did she hurt you?" asked Hugh, hurrying over. "I forgot about you—I'm sorry. Can you get up?"

"I'll try," said Rae in a dazed voice. "But before I get on to my feet—if I ever do—was that a *bath chair* I saw?"

"An 'lectric chair," explained Alan. "She's got a car, the old piece of cheese, but she only uses it sometimes. All the time, mostly, she goes bowling about in this thing. The first time, she knocked over our cabbages—"

"Caulis," corrected Hugh. "Twelve cauliflowers we had in the cart, and she knocked 'em all over the road."

"Didn't she stop?" asked Rae.

"She can't stop. How can she stop a thing like that in the middle of a hill? She gets in at the Castle at the top and she rolls down to the bottom, and if anything's in between, then—"

"Castle?" said Rae.

"Yes—she's the Duchess," said Alan. "Didn't you know?" He extended a hand. "Shall I pull you?"

"Not yet," said Rae faintly. "A Duchess in a bath chair wearing a polo topee knocked me down—is that it?"

" 'lectric chair. Has she hurt you?"

Rae got to her feet and felt herself.

"Two arms, two legs," she counted. "So far, so good. I think—"

"Your shoulder," said Hugh. "Look—she's hurt *that*."

Rae examined the damage. There was a slit at the top of her coat sleeve, and her shoulder ached a little.

"That's where the bath chair must have caught me," she said.

" 'lectric chair."

"Don't keep saying electric chair," said Rae with a touch of irritation. That's what they keep for murderers at Sing Sing or Dum Dum or Tom Tom or wherever the place is. That thing was a bath chair."

"You *push* a bath chair. This one's got a battery."

"Well, that's what hit me," said Rae. "I do hope that my friends are going to believe that I was hit by a Duchess in a polo topee in a bath chair with a battery—but it does sound a bit too much."

"Nobody likes her," said Alan as they resumed their journey. "Everybody thinks she's a piece of cheese, but she doesn't take any notice."

"Was she on her way to the market?"

"Dunno. But she owns nearly all of Thorpe—the woods; and the Castle and the village and everything."

"That's no reason why she should push me over," said Rae. "She doesn't own me. Is there any way I can get my own back on the old piece of cheese?"

"What we're doing," said Alan, "is making a cart like this one, only stronger, so's we can ride in it. Then we're going to wait till she passes, and then we'll push off and we'll catch her up—we'll be heavier, see? And then we'll see who can do the pushing."

"I'd like to be present," said Rae. "I'd like—oh!"

"What's the matter," asked Alan anxiously. "Is your shoulder—"

"No, it must be my head," said Rae. "The battery must have just glanced off it. I—I think I'm seeing things."

"Things? What things?"

"I thought I saw an angel," said Rae slowly. "A little, teeny, darling angel with blue eyes and a head of tight platinum curls and a rosebud mouth and—oh, look! its there again."

Hugh and Alan looked at her in alarm, and then followed her pointing finger, their expressions changing swiftly to disgust.

"Oh, Bi-an-KER," said Hugh furiously. "I told you not to come."

The angel, three feet high and clad in blue dungarees,

climbed purposefully into the cart.

"And your shoe," shouted Alan in exasperation. "Your shoe, Bi-an-KER. Where've you lost your shoe?"

The angel, looking surprised, stuck both feet out in front of her.

"There'th *one*," she said, and shifted her gaze to the bare toes of the other foot. "Where'th the other?"

"That's what I'm *asking,* you silly little fathead," said Alan furiously. "Which way did you come?"

The angel waved a tiny hand north by north-west.

"She came by the bridge," said Hugh resignedly. "That means we'll never find it."

Rae withdrew her eyes reluctantly from the enchanting vision lolling nonchalantly in the cart.

"Some relation?" she enquired.

"Sister," said Hugh without pride. "Bianca."

"Gee-up, gee-up, gee-up," shouted Bianca impatiently.

"Gee-up."

"We'll gee-up when we want to," said Hugh. "You shut up."

The tiny rosebud of a mouth opened and a piercing scream issued from it. Having released this steam, Bianca gave a seraphic smile and lay back to await transport.

"How old is she?" asked Rae in awe.

"Five," grunted Hugh, preparing to pull the cart homeward.

Men and Angels

"My puppy," said Bianca, settling to the motion, "got a bone and—"

"Pipe down," said Alan.

"My puppy—"

"Pipe down."

Bianca subsided, and the party turned into a narrow lane. Hugh opened a gate into a field, and Rae, looking beyond, saw a thatched farmhouse nestling in a hollow. They entered a yard, and Hugh, abandoning the cart and its occupant, led Rae straight into an enormous, red-floored kitchen. A stout woman looked up from the old-fashioned range, and Hugh led his guest forward.

"I say, Mart," he said, "we've brought a girl home."

The answer came in a rich, pleasant voice with more than a hint of London.

"At your time o' life!" Mart gave Rae a friendly wink. "What's your girl's name?"

"Rae—Rae, I've forgotten what," said Hugh.

"Mansfield," supplied Rae. "I'm sorry to come in like this, but—"

"You've gorn and torn your sleeve," said Mart, brushing aside non-essentials. "Those boys been rough?"

"Us? It was the Duchess."

"Oh—her. One of these days," promised Mart, "I'm going ter bring down a nice fat London policeman—fellow about my size—and stand him bang in the middle of that hill, and let's see the ole Duchess knock *him* down. He'd give her bath chair, I reckon—you staying for a meal ducks?"

"Well, if you and Mr. Selwyn don't—"

"Mr. Selwyn? Bless you, he don't know who's here and who's where. You can stay and welcome—want a wash or anything? Hughie'll show you. It's a long walk."

"This way," said Hugh. He led Rae into an outhouse and jerked his chin towards a sink.

"That's where you wash, if you want to," he said. "The towel's hanging up. And the other thing's over there—"

He waved airily at a distant shed. "Come back when you're ready."

Rae looked round at the evidences of a cluttered but carefree existence, and felt that she understood the reluctance of the boys to return to the formalities of school life. Making her way back to the kitchen after a simple but bracing clean-up, she made a shy offer of help.

"That's nice of you, ducks," said Mart. "Yes, you can lay yourself a place—the things are in that drawer there. We all eat together. And you can give that dog of yours a drink."

Rae performed these tasks, and Mart waved her to one of the hard kitchen chairs.

"Jest sit yourself down away from this 'ot fire, she said. "If there's anything you can do, I'll let you know. Won't be long before this lot's cooked, and then I can dish up. Where'd you fall in with the boys?"

Rae told her, and Mart nodded.

"I know the Lodge," she said. "I suppose the boys told you that the gardener comes courting?"

"Yes."

"He's past it, really," said Mart. She gave the fire a poke and blew out her cheeks. "Coo—it's hot. Fire in June don't seem right, really. But we've got to have hot water to get the dirt off them boys every night, and this thing's all I've got to cook on. Yes, he's past it, really, is the old chap, but he's only got that daughter of his, and I suppose he gets a bit lonely."

Rae studied the stout figure and liked what she saw. Mart was about fifty—short and extremely fat, but with a tight, trim look and an air of tirelessness. Her hair was grey, parted in the middle, and pinned in two plaits across her head; her eyes were brown and twinkling. Rae thought she had the wholesome air of the servants she had seen in pictures by Dutch artists. She found the brown eyes on her, and smiled.

"Bit lonely at the Lodge, won't it be, if you're there by yourself?"

"It's quiet," admitted Rae. "Before I met the boys to-day, I was feeling a bit—well, a little depressed."

"Why'd you come?" enquired Mart with simple and inoffensive directness. "What's become of Miss Ashton—isn't she home?"

"No. She's working quite near, though, and comes for week-ends."

"There's a brother come home from one of those places —Africa, or something."

In spite of herself, Rae felt her colour rising.

"Yes—Mr. Ashton's home," she said. "I mean, he's in England, but he isn't here."

"Well, he oughter be, if you're here, ducks," said Mart bluntly. "You don't leave a pretty girl like you with three old fogies like those up at the Lodge, not if you have any sense. Is 'e coming at all?"

"No," said Rae.

"Well, I shouldn't give up hope, if I was you. I know what men are—I wasn't married to Joe Harris for ten years for nothing. I suppose 'e said he was coming, and then left you to it?"

Rae tried hard to be offended, but there was a simple, motherly air about Mart which she found disarming. She gave a little smile of negation.

"I hardly know Mr. Ashton," she said gently. "Miss Ashton and I have been great friends for a long time—we were at school together."

"She s a young Tartar, she is. Comes here for eggs and milk when they're short—if you'll come and stir this, ducks, I can get on with something else."

Rae stirred the pleasant-smelling custard and poured it into a jug.

"Now we shan't be long," said Mart.

"Should I go out and meet Mr. Selwyn? He might think it

Men and Angels

odd if he comes in and finds me installed."

"He won't," promised Mart. "He goes about in a kind of 'appy dream, does Mr. Selwyn. Happiest man in England, he can't believe he's really here, half the time—it's like a luv'ly dream, only 'e don't have to wake up."

"The boys told me he liked the farm."

"Like it? He thinks it's Heaven, and so it is, compared with what he's had before. All those years shut up in an office—a man like 'im, fond of the open. And then to come to this. Mind you, he'll never be a farmer—not by a long chalk. He knows as much about farming as Bianca does, but there's men on the job, thank Gawd, that knows what they're doing—He dresses for the part, bless 'im—goes round wearing great thick boots and a Farmer Giles hat, but he can't dress up his pale little face and his specs—he looks like a prerfesser who's got into the wrong suit."

"Did you come here with him?"

"Me? No—Reeny and I came when he'd been here a month or two. Nearly fell back when I saw him—I was expecting a burly farmer and—well, you'll see what I mean when he comes in. When I got over my surprise, I said to myself, 'Mart,' I said, 'Mart ole girl, this place is the one. This is the job you've looked for for seven years. This is a permanent,' I said—and it was. We shan't leave here, Reeny and I, till Mr. Selwyn dies—or till we do."

"Do you like it?" asked Rae shyly.

Mart poured a rich, brown gravy into a sauce-boat and turned to face her questioner. Her round, red face was serious; one strong arm, upraised, rested on the high mantelpiece.

"Yes, I like it, ducks," she said slowly. "I like it. I dunno whether you say you like something that's a shelter or a home or a—a sort of harbour. It's all those. I'd been trying to find a job for years—people would have been glad to have me, but they couldn't get round Reeny. She's got a little kink—but so's everybody, when you come to think of it. I've got plenty of kinks—so've you, I'll bet. I know people they call sane who act a lot queerer than Reeny."

There was a pause, and Rae found herself putting a halting question.

"Is Reeny—is she—"

"She's all right," said Mart. "And she's a fine worker—quick and neat, and keeps the house a treat. But she's been unlucky, that's all. She waited fifteen years for a chap—saved for 'im, worked for 'im... and then he upped and married somebody else. It happens to a lot of us, but most of us 'ave a good cry and look out for the next. But Reeny couldn't do that, pore girl, and I've looked after her ever since. We're cousins, but you'd never know it—she's real ladylike, is Reeny. Her family went up in the world, and mine stayed just where they was. Reeny never has to watch her aitches, like me."

"But is she—"

"She's as right as rain," said Mart, "till something reminds her. She goes about, 'appy and busy as a bird, till mealtimes, and then she gets the bell in her hand and rings it, and that sets 'er off."

"Why a—a bell?"

"She was a school-teacher. For nearly twenty years. That's enough to send anyone off their heads, without bein' crossed in love. And when Reeny rings the bell, it takes her back, see? She's back at school."

"But then—why let her ring it?"

"I wanted to stop 'er, but Mr. Selwyn said No. 'Let 'er ring it, he said, and it'll get something out of her system.' And there must be something in that, 'cos Reeny's been as right as rain since we came, and as 'appy as can be. It works out a treat; Mr. Selwyn leaves it all to us—the house, the work, the cooking, the boys and Bianca. We get the boys off to school and buy their clothes for 'em and pack for 'em and send 'em off and pay their school bills. And he walks about 'is farm with that look of bliss on 'is face—makes me warm up every time I look at 'im. I often wonder whether I should've saddled 'im with three kids, but look how happy they are, bless 'em."

Rae stared.

"S-saddled him with—"

"Yes, I did. Put the chairs round, ducks, will you? I'm going to dish up."

Rae put a hand on a chair, but did not move, and Mart saw the interest in her face. "Go on—round they go, dearie."

"But how did you—"

"I'm just telling you. Just before I come 'ere, I went after a job in Croydon. A Mrs. Moore. I saw at once it wouldn't do—small house, no room for Reeny. But I liked Mrs. Moore, and I liked her kids. When I got settled here, I couldn't get 'er out of my head. Here's him, I said to myself, here's him all alone on this spanking place with nobody to spend all 'is money on, and there's her all alone with those three kids in that box of a house. So I told him about her, and what a lonely widow she was—I didn't bring in the kids, 'cos it might 'ave made him think twice. I asked her to come down for a day and see 'ow nicely I'd got settled with Reeny, and soon she came down again with the kids—and then again and again and then 'e married her. I often think 'e did it all in that dream of his, but they were happy. It didn't last long for 'er, pore thing, but when she died, she was glad to know the kids were safe. I often think—"

Mart broke off to shout loudly at three dogs—"Now then, you lot, you 'op it. Go on—'op off. We don't want you round at mealtimes. Out, Nelson! Go on, Blake, get out!"

"What's the other one?" asked Rae.

"Drake. Sailors, an' they behave like it. Go out and see where those boys are, ducks, will you?"

Rae went outside and saw the boys, closely followed by Bianca, coming towards the house. Some distance behind them came a small, thin man, and Rae had no difficulty in identifying him. She looked incredulously at the workmanlike clothes, the pale, rather weak face, the pince-nez balanced precariously…

She went to meet him, and held out a hand.

"How do you do," she said. "My name's Rae Mansfield and I—the boys very kindly—"

"Goood, goood," cooed Mr. Selwyn, looking at her with a kind, nervous smile.

"And Mart has very kindly—"

"Goood, goood."

"It's most awfully kind of you to—"

"Goood, goood," purred Mr. Selwyn, rubbing his hands. "Ah—lunch!"

Rae turned and saw a thin, tall woman at the door of the kitchen. She wore a clean white overall, and her hair was taken into a neat bun at the top of her head. Her face was serene, and she smiled pleasantly at her employer.

"Time to eat, Mr. Selwyn."

"Goood, Reeny, goood."

Reeny reached above her and took a large bell from a hook. She rang it vigorously for several moments, and the serene expression gradually gave way to one of the utmost severity. In a voice utterly unlike the one which she had used a moment ago, she rasped a command.

"All in line, all in line," she shouted. "Sharp, now—line up."

Hugh and Alan took their places near the kitchen door. Bianca, sucking a straw, strolled to her place beside them.

Mr. Selwyn, beckoning Rae to follow, stood in line beside them.

"Stand straight, now," shrieked Reeny. "Heads up, chins up, shoulders back, hands straight to the side. You there—Roddy—straight."

Alan straightened.

"Doris, what're you eating? Take it out at once."

Bianca, with the utmost calm, removed the straw. The martinet moved down the line and stopped before Rae.

"You a new girl?"

"Y-yes."

"You're too tall—move into place behind that boy there."

Rae moved.

"Attention, mark time, left right, left right, left *right,* left *right,* left turn."

The family turned.

"Left right, all together, left right, left right, now inside, quick *march*."

The family marched.

Chapter Seven

When Rae returned to the Lodge that evening, her dread of the next three weeks had vanished. Hugh and Alan escorted her to the garden gate, and Rae, humming a tune, strolled up the garden, looking with a new interest at the strawberry beds.

She glanced at her watch as she entered the house; the dressing bell must have gone, but she had ample time in which to put on the silk dress. On coming down to the drawing-room she found the members of the household in a state which would not have been noticed at the flat but which on this calm surface made a distinct ripple. Lady Ashton, on her way upstairs to put on the grey lace, had heard the telephone and come down again. It was Judy, she told Rae, and Judy had made the extraordinary suggestion that she was to sit for her portrait.

"Had she said anything of the sort to you?" she asked.

"Well, yes, she did mention it," said Rae. "She felt it would be a good opportunity to get hold of Mr. Ferris. She was going to do it for a present for Richard, and she was going to bring Mr. Ferris over at week-ends."

"That, I think, was her original intention," said Lady Ashton. "But it seems that she's changed her mind about giving it to Richard—she says I'm to keep it, which is very kind. And Mr. Ferris can't manage the week-ends, because he goes out with the students; he's only free on Wednesdays and Fridays, so Judy finds she has to drive him out here to-morrow and leave him for the day—she has to go back herself, of course, and that means two journeys for her, which is rather upsetting."

"You mean, this feller'll be here all day tomorrow?" demanded the General.

"I'm afraid so. It's really a little inconvenient, because it's going to be difficult to keep the meals running smoothly. I—"

"Oh, you mustn't worry about that, Dorothy," put in Miss Beckwith. "We shall plan the whole thing tonight, and I shall see that there's no hitch of any kind. I know very well how everything needs to be done."

The General, satisfied that his comfort was to be attended to, lost his look of strain, but remained dissatisfied.

"You'll never," he told his sister, "get as good a portrait done by one of these modern johnnies as that one Ambrose Fitzroy did of Mother."

"Well, no that really was a charming one—you remember it, Blanche? Bertram, you must show it to Rae one of these days."

The gong sounded and the party moved into the dining-room.

Men and Angels

"Where're you going to put the feller?" asked the General. He'll ask for a north light—they always ask for a north light. I suppose the old playroom's really the place."

"I thought of the little reading-room upstairs," said Lady Ashton.

"That would do, I suppose. What did you say his name was?"

"Ferris. Aylmer Ferris. I think I've heard it somewhere or seen it, perhaps."

"More than I have," said the General. "People tell you that this or that feller's famous, and when you come down to it, nobody's ever heard of them. Can't say I want to see one of those artist johnnies all over the house—never could stand those ridiculous pinafores they wear, like a musical comedy ploughboy. Ambrose didn't have to dress up and look the part—he simply turned out a first-rate picture, and none of this stuff to impress the observer. I remember that dreadful feller, Holmwood, who strutted about in this very room at Estelle's wedding."

"He was a musician, wasn't he?" asked Miss Beckwith.

"Estelle told me he was a great artist, when I asked her."

The General looked at Rae with a twinkle, and she braced herself for the joke. "Said to her, 'Great artist? Then how can anyone know, if he comes here without his pinafore?' Ha ha ha."

Rae gave a very creditable little laugh, and the General

went on with his dinner in great good humour, almost reconciled to the morrow's upsetting prospect.

Judy drove up to the house before ten o'clock next morning and the General went into the hall to receive the guest. Mr. Ferris was a tall, trim gentleman in the late thirties, looking, in a sports jacket and grey flannel trousers, so ordinary and inartistic as to arouse the General's deepest suspicions. Mr. Ferris's behaviour rapidly changed the suspicion to dislike. There was no polite lingering and no exchange of small talk. Having made a brief bow to the three ladies in the drawing-room, the artist approached his sitter. Wordlessly, he examined her face, walking round to observe it from every angle. This inspection over, he looked round the room with a frown of disapproval.

"Is the sitting," he asked, "to take place here?"

"Oh no." Lady Ashton, though a little puzzled, was still placid. "We thought you might like to use one of the rooms upstairs—would you care—"

"Let us go up," said Mr. Ferris.

He followed Lady Ashton up the stairs, and Miss Beckwith went up after them. The General, after staring at the visitor's receding back with a frown, stumped upstairs in the rear. Judy and Rae were alone.

"Rae"—Judy swung round and studied her friend's face intently—"are you all right? Has it been too frightful to bear, all this?" She waved a hand vaguely round the room. "I've been wondering whether you'd decide to kick the whole thing over and go back to Town. What're you smiling at? You don't *like* it?"

At the incredulous tone, Rae smiled more widely.

"I'm very happy, thank you," she said calmly. "I've found a whole colony of friends."

"Where—here?"

"Thorpe Farm."

"Thorpe Farm?" Judy frowned. "Thorpe Farm—name of Selwyn or something, isn't it? Used to be a schoolmaster—that one?"

"It's too long a story if you've got to get back," said Rae. "What time do you come back for Mr. Ferris?"

Judy ran her hands through her hair, making it stand up stiffly.

"Oh, Lord, I dunno," she said wearily. "I wish I'd never got started on the beastly thing. It was only because I thought that Richard would like it—and I thought that if the price was too high for me, I could have asked him to pay something towards it. But now I've decided that Richard isn't going to have it, and that'll mean paying for it myself. He's charging me forty pounds."

"Judy! Good heavens!"

"Don't say good heavens in that tone—it's cheap at the price. You've got to remember that he's a well-known and successful artist—you don't imagine that he does all his princes and potentates for a miserable fee like forty pounds, do you? Of course he doesn't! But the whole thing's gone wrong; I thought Richard would be paying half, and I thought he'd be here and I could bring this Ferris at weekends and take him back with me and—oh! it was all going to work out wonderfully. And now look! I'm driving to and fro like a scalded cat, and you're stuck here alone and—oh! what's the use?" she sighed. "Come on upstairs for a minute, Rae, and lend me a comb."

Standing before Rae's dressing-table, Judy got her hair into order, while Rae, in a way that would have distressed Miss Beckwith very much, lay on the smooth bedspread, watching idly.

"Did Rose send you an invitation to that party of hers?" Judy asked.

"She may have done, but I suppose it went to the flat," said Rae.

"Well I got one—in spite of having told her we'd both be out of town. It's on Thursday—tomorrow. I supposed she wants us to go and see Richard dancing on her train."

"*In* her train."

"Round her train. In and out of her blasted train. The girl's got a hell of a nerve, Rae—pale-blue invitation card, all done up with golden letters and—wait! It's in my bag—I'll show you."

Heads together, they looked at the blue-and-gold card.

"At her age—she's not more than four months older than I am—and with a bit part," said Judy in a voice of bitter scorn.

Men and Angels

"Who does she think she is, throwing parties at smart hotels? I'd give something to know who was doing the paying, so I would!"

"Doesn't it all come under what they call publicity?"

"She runs her own publicity—don't you worry." Judy gave the card a contemptuous spin and sent it flying across the room. She glanced at the clock and picked up her bag hastily."

"I'm off," she said. "Oh—lend me some money, Rae—I'll give it to you tonight, but I didn't bring any with me—where d'you keep it?" Rae nodded towards the drawer, and Judy, opening it and taking out a hand-bag, extracted a note-case. "I'll take a couple of pounds." She pulled them out an a visiting card fluttered out with them and dropped to the floor. "Sorry!" she said, stooping to pick it up. "Here it—"

She stopped, her eyes on the card, her brows drawn together in a puzzled frown. Rae spoke calmly.

"It's only one of Uncle Fabian's," she said. "You can tear it up—I must have kept it for the address or something."

"B-but it says Sir Fabian Hollis, Bart. You mean, he's a—a *baronet*?"

Rae looked puzzled in her turn.

"Of course he's a baronet," she said. He s always been a baronet—well, I mean for about twenty—no, about eighteen years. You always knew he was."

"But I *didn't!*" exclaimed Judy, her eyes wide and, Rae thought, a little blank. "I didn't! I couldn't understand all that bit about how women all got bowled over, old *and* young. I could understand the old, but I always thought to myself, when you said the girls went for him, that you'd somehow got it wrong—over forty, after all, was over forty and—"

"And my Uncle Fabian, at over forty," said Rae, unmoved "can make all the men we go out with look like schoolboys. I think that even if you put him beside—beside Richard, you'd see that—"

"Oh, Rae!"

It was a long, breathless cry. Rae saw that Judy was staring at her, her bag slipping to the floor and her hands clinging to the rails of the old-fashioned bed "Oh ... Rae! ..."

There was a long silence. Judy had obviously thought of something—what it was, Rae had no idea, and strove for a few moments to guess. Unsuccessful, she spoke:

"What is it?"

"Your uncle."

"My uncle?"

"Yes. Rae"—Judy leaned forward and spoke crisply and urgently—"talk fast—I haven't much time. You said your uncle's a killer?"

"A—"

"Oh—a *lady*-killer. Is he *really* a—a Casanova?"

"In a way."

"Good-looking?"

"Very."

Men and Angels

"Smart? I mean—man-about-town? I mean—"

"Well-groomed? Yes. I told you-he looks like those advertisements in magazines—he really is awfully impressive."

"Rich?"

"No—enough for himself in a very comfortable way, but nothing over to be generous with and leave himself short—why all this, Judy?"

"Wait a minute. Now listen *carefully*. You say he's the very devil with young actresses?"

"Dev—"

"*Oh!*" Judy made an impatient movement. You say he likes actresses, and that they really do go for him?"

"Yes. But—"

"Don't but anything," said Judy, standing up with a sudden air of calm decision. "Hand me that card."

"Uncle Fabian's?"

"Yes. And now"—Judy swooped swiftly and retrieved the blue-and-gold invitation—"got an envelope?" she asked.

"Yes, but—"

"Oh, Rae," cried Judy, "I'm in a *hurry*! I've got to get back to that blasted school. Give me an envelope and then read me out your uncle's address."

"But—"

"If you say but again," said Judy fiercely, "I'll scream. There's no but in the case. We're sending your uncle to Rosanna Lee's party."

"But—I mean—you can't!"

"I have," said Judy at the writing-table, printing a block capital address on the envelope. "He's going, is Uncle Fabian, to her party. There! That's that. Got a stamp?"

Rae, wordless, produced a stamp, and Judy stuck it on and tucked in the flap of the envelope. "Now I'll drop that into a postbox on my way back, and then we'll sit back and see what the explosion throws up. Where's my bag?—oh, there."

She was at the door. Rae, standing in the middle of the room, took a step forward.

"Don't come down," said Judy. "And don't try to argue or anything. If I'd only had the least bit of sense, Rae, I should never have let you get stuck down here while Richard danced round with Madame Soublin's most notable failure. All I had to do was to put your Uncle Fabian somewhere nearby, and Rosanna would have taken him at his face value and attached herself to him at once. But I didn't dream.... You misled me, you see, by telling me everything about him *except* the one fact that would have put all the rest into place and explained his success with the young and lovelies. You left out his title. Rosanna has seen plenty of good-looking men; she's even known good-looking men with Rolls-Royces. But perhaps she doesn't know so many man who are good-looking and who have an impeccably-groomed air *and* a Rolls-Royce *and* a title. It gives that little bit of extra weight that sends the scales down. Our Rosanna's background isn't so secure that she can throw off baronets without thought. They're not so great a prize when you compare them with what some actresses grab, but then, Rosanna's only beginning. When Fabian gets this invitation, I'm pretty sure he'll go to that party; if he goes, I'm pretty sure that Rosanna will see all his possibilities. If she does, and if she shows Richard she does, I'm absolutely sure of this: that'll be the end, as far as Richard is concerned. I'm not as well up in my brother's character as I once thought I was, but I know one thing about him well, and it's this: he won't stay up there to go shares with a middle-aged charmer. He'll—"

"One moment, Judy," broke in Rae quietly.

Judy, at the door, paused and looked round.

"Well?"

"If you're doing this to detach Richard from Rosanna—"

"I am."

"If you're doing it on my account, I'd very much rather you left things as they are."

Judy studied her for a few moments without speaking.

"You mean," she said at last, "that you don't care one way or the other?"

Rae made an effort and spoke steadily.

"That's what I mean," she said. "I don't care—one way or the other."

"I see. Well, I don't blame you," said Judy, "but that's your own affair. This is mine. I owe Richard something for getting you down here for nothing. I'm going to send this invitation. I don't know what'll come of it, but I know that it's going to make me feel a whole lot better. Good-bye, Rae."

The door banged. Rae stood still, staring at it.

Chapter Eight

It was obvious that Mr. Ferris thought very little of the room upstairs, but, beyond giving a disparaging glance round it and making a few adjustments to the heavy velvet curtains, he made no comment. Turning to his hostess, he addressed her in his polite but scarcely warm manner.

"Perhaps," he said, "you will show me some of your dresses."

At this extraordinary suggestion, the General gave the artist a glare in which his dislike and suspicion were openly declared.

"Show you?"

"Something blue, if you've got it," proceeded Mr. Ferris, ignoring the interruption. "Something of the shade of this lining here—or perhaps approaching that cushion. If you bring them, we'll choose something."

"Oh! Oh yes, I'll go and bring you a few to look at," said Lady Ashton.

"And a shawl," added Mr. Ferris.

"A shawl? I never wear a shawl," said Lady Ashton in

surprise. "I think I'd look a little odd in a—"

"To drape; to drape behind you." Mr. Ferris was obviously exercising the greatest patience and self-control. "And a screen, perhaps. Have you a screen?"

"I've got a very good screen," said the General. "Chinese. Carved."

"No colour," commented Mr. Ferris.

"Colour? It's got some magnificent colour," declared the General. "All its panels are full of colour—the finest colour you've"—there was a perceptible accent on the word "ever seen. I've got a picture of my mother painted against it—done by Ambrose Fitzroy—a fine piece of work."

"If somebody would fetch the screen," said Mr. Ferris coldly, "I could decide whether it would make a suitable background."

"I'll fetch it," said the General. "It's in my study."

He went along the corridor leading to his own part of the house and, entering the study, seized the screen and folded it. Lifting it was a difficult feat, but the General, supported by the thought of opening it with a flourish before the artist, bore it resolutely, if on a somewhat zigzag course, towards the studio. Mr. Ferris, receiving it coolly, pulled it to a place near the window and, hanging a shawl and dress upon it, studied the effect from several angles.

"I'll use it," he said finally. "Now, if you will kindly sit here"—he motioned Lady Ashton to a chair—"I shall decide how I shall paint you."

He walked to and fro in silence, studying the effect of first one and then another dress against Lady Ashton. Lost in his work, rearranging the folds, draping fabric, he awoke at last to the fact that Miss Beckwith and the General were still in the room, watching his movements with wholehearted interest. With the utmost politeness, but without any attempt to disguise his purpose, he shepherded them both to the door and shut it after them. The General, breathing heavily, stood on the threshold and looked as though he was going to kick it open again.

"I think," said Miss Beckwith hurriedly, "I'll see about the meals—do you think Mr. Ferris will be staying to dinner?"

The General made no response. He joined Rae, who was coming slowly downstairs, and walked down beside her.

"If Judy had said a word to me before she started this tomfoolery," he said, "I could have given her a word of warning about these fellers. He's up there now, stepping up and down on his toes like a ballet dancer, with his eyes half shut and his head on one side, but if he thinks that sort of thing takes me in, he's making a mistake. I knew what a good painting was long before he came into the world, and for all his posturing, I'll warrant you he doesn't turn out half such a good finished article as Ambrose Fitzroy did with half the fuss. You wait and see—not looking forward to my lunch, with that jackanapes at the table," he ended gloomily.

When lunch-time came, however, Mr. Ferris, working

steadily and silently, was unwilling to stop. He had a perfect model—Lady Ashton was rising rapidly in his estimation, so amenable, so placid was she—and so silent. Rae, who had come upstairs to find out why they were keeping the General from his lunch, had to go down again with a request from Mr. Ferris for coffee and sandwiches.

"Does he think," the General demanded of Miss Beckwith, "does he think he can keep Dorothy up there all these hours on coffee and sandwiches? Does he?"

"The best thing we can do," said Miss Beckwith sensibly, "is to give him exactly what he wants, and do exactly as he asks, and then in that way we shall be rid of him soonest. Doesn't he remind you a little of poor Mark Hewling, who went down in that ship crossing to the Isle of Man?"

The General made no response, but the question seemed to cheer him; he walked into lunch with Rae, and Miss Beckwith went out to the kitchen to order the sandwiches.

Mr. Ferris left before dinner. Judy came over to fetch him, but did not come into the house. Rae went down the steps and leaned against the car door, talking.

"How did you get on yesterday?" asked Judy. "Mother said you spent the day out. Walking, she said, but I bet you didn't walk. Except to Thorpe Farm, of course."

"I got knocked over by a bath chair," said Rae, not without pride.

"Good Lord—the Duchess?"

"Yes."

"Did she stop?"

"No. She called me a silly gel. Could I sue her for a new coat?—She tore the shoulder."

"You could sue her, but it wouldn't do you any good. She's a horrid bit of work. Did you tell Uncle Bertram?"

"No."

"Well, don't. The very mention of the Duchess upsets his liver—they loathe each other. *She* despises him and thinks he's a weak-kneed escapist and *he* thinks she's a cunning old bitch, though no Fitzroy could bring himself to use the word, especially of a lady. You see, she keeps going on at him for letting the servant problem drive him out of his house."

"Did it?"

"Yes. He believed in the old kind—print gowns, white caps— the sort that got on with the work and didn't obtrude — do I mean obtrude? yes—didn't obtrude their personalities— or their problems. When they died out, he gave up, but not the Duchess. She didn't have a mere ten-bedroom Manor like the Fitzroys—she had a forty-room Castle to keep going, and she keeps it going, too. It's the only ancestral home in England that isn't either all shut up, or half shut up, or thrown open to the public, or handed over to whatever that Trust is that takes them. What's its name?"

"Never mind its name—go on about the Duchess."

"Well, she gets all the servants she wants. She engages

them herself, gives them a pittance instead of a proper wage, and stipulates that they must stay six months. At the end of the six months, she writes two lines in her own fair hand on her own embossed notepaper—she just says this flunkey or varlet or whoever he or she was—has worked for me for six months—that s all. Just that bare statement. And on that recommendation they can get jobs wherever they like, and at any salary they like. It's like a rosette at the horse show— you get it pinned on you and you take it home and it's yours for ever."

"But I don't see why her recommendation should have more weight than—"

"You've *seen* her, haven't you?" demanded Judy. "She's knocked you down and ruined your garments and rolled on regardless? Well, that's a good sample of her behaviour. She rolls over everybody. And she's so awful that six months in her service is regarded as a—well, as a terrific test. Anyone that survives it is made for life. It isn't only because they've come through it—it's because during those six months they've seen service of the highest sort. The castle's always full of the bluest blood—the very bluest. Six months there means six months of serving kings and princes. They just finish bowing out one when the next drives up. So you see why they're so sought-after when they've done their awful probation?"

"Yes. Do the princes ever borrow the bath chair?"

"No—that's exclusively Duchess. Did you like her wonderful topee? One of these days she's going to hear that Aylmer Ferris is here, and she'll come bowling down—she likes to keep in with the Arts—she can't quite make up her mind whether she'd rather be hostess to a prince or patroness to a poet—here's Mr. Ferris. I posted that thing, Rae."

"Was it wise?"

"The very highest wisdom," said Judy. "See you on Friday."

Rae went upstairs for what she now called Operation Silk Frock, and passed the open door of the room in which the sittings were taking place. The General, standing moodily in front of the easel, called to her as she went by.

"Come in, come on in," he invited. "Come and tell me what you think of it."

Rae looked; there was not much to see, and she thought it too early for the General to look gloomy.

"It's hard to judge yet" she began.

"I don't think much of it," growled the General. "Look at that vase beside her. Look at the real thing, I mean there it is. Now look at the shape he's made it—d'you call that a reproduction of the thing he was looking at?"

"Well, they don't always—"

"Quite so, quite so. They don't always paint what they see. They paint a teapot upside down and call it Sunset, or Obsession, or Frustration or some such. But if a man's going to paint a portrait, is he going to paint what he's asked to paint, or is he going to daub away at something that's got into his eye?"

In Rae's opinion, which she did not voice, they could only

wait and see.

"Wait here," said the General suddenly. "Just wait here a minute and I'll bring you something that'll show you I'm not merely carping. Now wait here—I won't be long."

He returned with a large framed portrait under his arm. Propping it against the back of a chair, he led Rae up to it.

"Look there now," he said. "That's my mother—Judy's grandmother. Old Ambrose Fitzroy painted that against the same screen. Look at the screen—every detail as sharp as life. Look at that face—it might be my mother sitting there. No drapery and no fuss—he just put her against the screen and painted 'em both—like it?"

"It's most awfully like Lady Ashton," said Rae. "It's almost exactly like her."

"Well, yes, she's like her mother," admitted the General. "I'm not quite sure how old my mother was when that was painted, but she'd be about the same age, perhaps. Yes, they're alike. None of the children took after her—pity. But I value that picture very highly, and if this painter johnny can produce anything half as good as this is, I'll make him a handsome apology, upon me soul I will. But I don't think I'll have to."

Rae went to her room and dressed. She went downstairs to find Miss Beckwith coming away from the telephone.

"It's for you," she said.

Rae's heart gave a bound, and she had a second's wild hope of hearing Richard's voice. Before she reached the in-

Men and Angels

strument, however, she had pulled herself together and put the possibility firmly aside. She picked up the receiver and heard a childish voice.

"Rae?"

"Yes."

"This is Alan. Will you come swimming to-morrow?"

"I'd love to. Thank you. Where?"

"Oh—just swimming," said Alan. "Have you brought a bathing costume, Mart says, 'cos if not she says you can borrow Hugh's trunks and she can fix you up a sun-suit sort of top."

"Well, I might get one here—there's a girl of my own age and—"

"No," said Alan. "I mean, don't borrow one."

"Why on earth not?"

"Because—well, if you asked them to lend you one, they might say where were you swimming, and p'raps they wouldn't like you to swim if you told them you were going to, 'cos some people don't, do they? If you just said you were coming to see us, you could come without any bathing suit and then we'd—"

Throughout this circumlocution, Rae's mind worked swiftly. They were obviously going to swim in forbidden waters—the General had mentioned something... had closed something.... But a swim was a swim, reflected Rae, and the less she knew of prohibitions, the better it would be for all swimmers.

"What time?" she asked, breaking in upon Alan's monologue.

"Mart says to come early and have lunch, and then we'll go swimming afterwards."

"It's a date."

"That's good," said Alan, with flattering sincerity. "But if I were you, I wouldn't say anything about—"

"I never say anything about anything," said Rae. "It's a way I've got. Good-bye."

"Good-bye."

Chapter Nine

Rae awoke next morning to find rain—the first since her arrival at Thorpe—pattering against the windowpanes. Swimming seemed a less likely and certainly a less attractive proposition than it had done the previous evening. By the middle of the morning, the showers had settled to a steady downpour, and Rae went to the telephone to cancel the day's engagement with Hugh and Alan.

"Will you come tomorrow instead?" asked Hugh.

Rae hesitated; Judy was to come home on Friday, but it was unlikely that she would arrive before dinner—she had to take Mr. Ferris back after the sitting.

"I'll come if it's fine," she promised.

It proved to be fine indeed. Rae, who had spent the previous day reading in the drawing-room, sniffed the cool, fresh air, and walked briskly in the direction of the farm. Reading, she conceded, was all very well, but people ought to have books that people could read. Lady Ashton had offered her *Ethics of the Dust* and thrown in *Don Quixote* as light relief; Miss Beckwith had brought her two volumes entitled *Disas-*

ters of the Deep, and the General, finding her gazing out into the dripping garden, had led her, with the utmost kindness, into the library and personally selected three volumes: *Gulliver's Travels, Bacon's Essays* and *The Swiss Family Robinson.* Surrounded by these excellent works, Rae passed the day in misery, looking out at the downpour, and finding her only comfort in the recollection that Mrs. Noah had put up with several weeks of it.

The farm was in sight; Hugh and Alan were approaching, Mart was waving a duster from an upper window; Bianca, wearing one shoe and swinging the other, was on her way across the field to meet Rae. The sun shone, and spirits were high.

Swimming took place after lunch, and Rae, keeping to her resolve to ask no questions, followed without comment the boys' wide detour round the Thorpe Lodge property and the subsequent double back in the direction of what was clearly a Thorpe Lodge field. The gate was padlocked, but Hugh passed it by without pause and, straddling the ditch a little farther on, stooped and removed a neatly-cut-out piece of hedge.

"Go on," he said, with a jerk of his chin.

Alan scrambled through; Rae handed over Bianca and followed; Hugh came last and filled up the hedge. In single file, with every appearance of innocence but with a certain caution in keeping close to the sheltering fence, the four went on until they reached a gate. This, too, was stoutly padlocked; Hugh gave the bottom bar a twist and escorted his charges through, replacing the bar after them. Rae saw that they had come to a sudden widening of the river, and drew a deep breath as she stood on the bank and looked about her.

It was a perfect little pool in a perfect setting. Encircled by trees, with a tiny waterfall at one end, the water glistened in the sun, sparkling and clear. A tree stump near the water's edge made a convenient diving board. As Rae looked round, enchanted, Alan emerged from the bushes which had served as a dressing-room and plunged into the water. Hugh went next, and Bianca, dancing to and fro in excitement, waved her diminutive bathing suit at Rae.

"Come on and thwim, come on and thwim," she urged.

"Well, come on," said Rae. "Come and undress in this woody bit."

Bianca slipped off the shoulder-straps of her dungarees and sat on the ground to pull them off. Rae, absorbed in the problem of adjusting the two badly matching pieces of her borrowed suit, forgot her companion until, hearing a yelp of glee, she looked up. Bianca was walking steadily towards the water; as Rae watched, she marched on without pause, descended the bank, stepped into the river and vanished.

It took only a few seconds for Rae to plunge in, seize an arm and a strap and haul her in to the side. Patting his sister vigorously on the back, Alan addressed her in angry tones.

"What d'you think you're trying to be?" he demanded, "A submarine?"

"Why did she do it?" asked Rae, still breathless with fright. "Has she ever done that before?"

"She's never been before," said Hugh calmly. "I suppose she just thought she could do it, like us."

"I thwam," announced Bianca, between splutters. "I did thwim."

"You didn't, you silly little fathead," denied Alan. "You've got to stay on *top* of the water if you want to swim."

"I thwam on the bottom," explained Bianca.

"But that's no good, don't you see?" pointed out Rae. "You've got to learn how to—"

"You've got to wriggle your hands and feet about, and then you won't sink," explained Hugh. "Now look—I'll throw in that fat branch and you've got to hang on to it—see? If you let go, you'll go down again. Come on. Now hang on and twiddle your feet and you'll—your *feet*, I said, not your hands. You've got to hang on with your hands. Got it? Well, don't let go."

He gave the craft a push, and Bianca was launched. The curls clinging damply round her head, two tiny hands clutching the knots of the branch, she performed a slow circle in the middle of the river and then let go and sank. The three watchers dived together and effected a rescue.

"You look here," said Hugh angrily. "I'm not going to stay here all the time fishing you off the bottom. You either stay on top or you get out and stay out."

Men and Angels

"I'll stay with her," offered Rae.

"No—we're all going to dive," said Alan. "She'll be all right—look, I can see the stones at the bottom—we can't *lose* her. Come on. Now you hang on, Bianca."

"I thwam. I can make my legs go like—"

"All right—pipe down."

The rest of the afternoon passed without incident. Rae found that Bianca's submersions were invariably preceded by a triumphant 'I'm thwimming—look.' Her alarm was succeeded by astonishment at the amount of water Bianca could take in without apparent harm.

They dressed and drank the flask of hot cocoa which Mart had provided. Rae, wringing out her suit and swinging it to and fro to dry it, was surprised to see Alan clambering up a tree with Hugh's suit and his own.

"Chuck me up yours and Bianca's," he said, holding out n hand. "And the towels."

"What for?" asked Rae.

"We don't take 'em home any more now that it's warm enough to swim every day. We leave them up here so's people won't see—won't take 'em."

Rae, without further parley, threw up the two suits and saw him fasten them carefully to a leafy branch. Hugh, walking round the tree and surveying it from all angles, pronounced that nothing was visible.

"That's all right," said Alan, descending. "Do you know

how to get here direct, without coming to us first?" he asked Rae. "It's much shorter for you if you come on your own, and we could fix a time to meet you."

"I think I'd get here," said Rae. "Down the lane with the big oak, then the gap in the hedge—"

"And put it back *properly,* remember."

"—and then the gate. Yes, I think I know. But why all the precautions?" she asked. "Anybody who was taking a walk could just turn up suddenly while you were swimming."

"If it was anybody from the Lodge," said Alan, "then we'd hear a whistle."

Rae stared at him.

"What whistle?"

"Oh—just a sort of warning whistle."

"I see. Your friend the gardener, I take it?"

"Well, he's really Mart's friend," explained Alan. "Will you come tomorrow?"

"Not tomorrow, and not Sunday," said Rae, remembering Judy. "But Monday, if it's fine."

"Monday, then. If we walk back slowly," said Alan, who appeared to forget nothing, "your hair'll be nice and dry." Walking back slowly, Rae got to the Lodge to find the General going indoors after an afternoon's work in the greenhouse. He led her round to a side-door, indicating his out-at-elbows jacket and heavy boots.

"Mustn't go in the other way with these on," he said.

Men and Angels

"How far did you get to-day?"

"Far? Oh, I—well, I didn't get far at all, as a matter of fact. I went to lunch at the Farm again."

"Making friends? That's good," said the General. "I don't know much about the people down there. Fellow called Moore, I understand—I'm told he's not much of a farmer. Schoolmaster or something of the sort, I fancy. I suppose it's the girl you've met—his daughter."

"Well, yes."

"Couple of sons, too, I hear. Are they nice lads?"

"They're awfully nice," said Rae. "I don't see much of their father—he's really their stepfather, and his name is—"

"Stepfather, is he? I didn't know—if I'm not mistaken, that's Judy's car coming round—yes, I wish you'd ask her to hurry up and take that feller off. Coffee and sandwiches up there again to-day."

Rae met Judy and walked with her towards the house.

"Your uncle wants the painter fellow removed," she said.

"So do I," said Judy gloomily. "Can you tell me what made me think of this? I'm stuck in the transport business—to and fro, this way and that, coming, going, hither and thither—and what for? A portrait that Mother doesn't want, that Uncle's already got, and that Richard isn't jolly well going to get—did you remember about the party yesterday, Rae?"

"Yes." Rae spoke hesitatingly. "But I'm quite sure, Judy, that Uncle Fabian wouldn't have gone to it."

"Why not? These ambitious coming-on actresses send out invitations to anybody they think is going to be useful to them. He'll regard it as a sign of his popularity. He'll think Rosanna saw him somewhere and said, 'Tell me, who is that distinguished-looking man standing by that palm?'—Of course he'd go."

"I don't feel that he—"

"Look, Rae." Judy broke into the soft tones with an unusual seriousness in her own. "You and I don't feel the same way about this. You're—don't be offended but you're one of those people who let other people push you here and there without doing anything to push back. I'm not—and there's the difference. When I heard about Richard and Rosanna, I was nearly beside myself with rage and I thought that you would be, too, when I told you. But you weren't. I don't suppose you liked it, but you took it quietly and—and accepted it, and went on as if nothing had happened. I can't do that. I don't like to think that I harbour grudges, but I don't think it's right that Richard should put you down here to amuse him, and then calmly go off and amuse himself with someone else. It was a mean trick, and it needs—it needs paying off."

"He knew you were down here," pointed out Rae. "It wasn't as though I was to be entirely on my own."

"That's merely making excuses, and he doesn't—he really doesn't deserve that calm sort of acceptance of any treatment he cares to hand out, Rae. It *was* a mean trick, and you know it."

Men and Angels

"But I'm very happy, and I'm having a nice time and—"

"That's beside the point. I'm glad you are, even if I can't understand how you have found anything here to be happy about. I don't even understand how you could have—have stood up to Richard without—without getting bowled over, but thank heaven you did. Only—I'm not prepared to fold my hands meekly, like you, and let Richard get off scot-free. I suppose sending that invitation was childish and petty, and what Mother would call not the action of a lady, but ever since I posted it, I've felt better."

"Well, you needn't have done it on my account. I've told you—I'm perfectly happy."

"I'm glad. But that doesn't excuse Richard."

Rae walked to the car, shut Mr. Ferris in, and watched it out of sight. Passing the studio on her way upstairs, she saw the General, already changed, beckoning to her.

"Come in here a minute," he said. "Come and stand here and tell me what you think. Don't say anything yet—just take it in and then tell me what you think."

Rae joined him in front of the easel; together they gazed at the half-finished portrait.

"Now just answer my questions," said the General. "Is that a good likeness?"

"It's hard to say yet. What do you think?"

"I am not giving an opinion," said the General heavily. "I gave up saying what I think twenty years ago. Twenty years ago I could discuss a great many subjects frankly and openly with my friends, but most of my friends have gone now; the old world's gone, and if I utter an opinion in the new world, nobody knows what I'm talking about. So I say very little. But I'd be interested to know what you, with your young, your modern eye, can see in that. What, for example, do you call the object she's holding?"

Rae studied it.

"I can't quite say," she said at last. "It looks a little bit— it can't be, of course, but it does look like a flower-pot."

"A flower-pot—exactly!" The General's voice was husky with suppressed triumph. "When I laid eyes on it just now, I said, 'Good God, why on earth is she holding a flowerpot?' But you see, the point is that she isn't."

"Isn't holding it?"

"There is no flower-pot," pronounced the General. "She's holding that vase—the one you see over there. Now, look at that vase and tell me if you see the smallest resemblance between it and a flower-pot?"

"No—none."

"Quite so. Why? Because there is none. None whatsoever. And yet this fellow, this much-lauded portrait painter, whose work Judy tells me is acclaimed everywhere, is going to present us calmly with a face—anybody's face, because that looks like anybody's face—and a flower-pot, and we shall be expected to thank him. And what's more, we'll be expected to pay him. And what's worst of all, we shall be expected to like it. If we don't like it, we shall be pointed out as uncultured boors who don't understand a fine work of art when we see it. I'm relieved, my dear, very much relieved, to hear you say that it's a flower-pot. Now wait here for a moment—I'll go along and get Ambrose Fitzroy's picture again and we'll compare the two."

Rae waited, and the old work was placed beside the new. "Now compare them," invited the General. "One is a woman holding a vase—we might almost say it's my sister holding a vase, the resemblance is so striking. Now look at the other. A blur that's the Chinese screen, mark you—a confused blur of colours, and look what Ambrose made of the same screen—you see? This feller gives us a blur, a face—I'll go as far as to admit it's a face of some sort—and a flower-pot."

Rae stood silent, pleased to provide an outlet for the old man's anger. She cared little whether Lady Ashton held a vase or a flower-pot, or whether the portrait was good or bad; she was not a judge, and she was not much interested. But she could listen while the General worked off a little steam. So much better did he feel after it that he placed the Fitzroy carefully behind the bookcase and prepared to follow Rae downstairs. Lady Ashton and Miss Beckwith, changed and coming in from a last glance at the arrangements for dinner, met them in the hall.

"Here we all are," said Lady Ashton. "You've both been looking at the picture, I expect?"

"Just glancing, just glancing," said the General. "Where's

Judy—not back yet?"

"She won't be long, I expect," said Lady Ashton. "Here she is now—I hear the car."

The car stopped at the door, and the General walked forward to admit his niece.

"Well, Judy," he began, and stopped. "God bless my soul!" he exclaimed. "Hello Richard!"

Richard stepped into the hall and dropped two suitcases on the floor.

"Hello sir. Hello, Miss Beckwith—how smart you all look. Hello, Mother." He stooped to kiss his mother's cheek, and then took two more leisurely steps and, putting his hands on the frozen Rae's shoulders, bent and kissed her firmly on the lips.

"My dear Miss Mansfield," he said. "Fancy meeting you here!"

Chapter Ten

Dinner that night was not the usual sedate function to which Rae had become accustomed. Since Richard had given no notice of his coming, extra food had to be prepared; since he had not come alone, two places had to be added to the meal. The serious looking Edward, who had come, Richard informed them, for the weekend, stood talking to the General in the hall while the bustle of preparation went on around them.

"I suppose," said the General, "you're glad to be back in England."

"Yes, sir—rather, sir" said Edward.

"Used to feel the same myself every time I got back. Always used to feel, somehow, that there was something in the air I could recognise —blindfold me, I used to say, and put me down in one country after another, and I'll tell you the minute I smell England."

This unusual way of recognising the mother country had obviously not struck Edward before, and he turned involuntarily to the open hall door and sniffed tentatively the English air.

"Clean sort of smell," said the General. "Smell of home, somehow—I suppose you've got a busy programme for your leave?"

Edward attempted to give some hint of the joys before him, but found Lady Ashton waiting to take him to his room and followed her upstairs. Richard produced from the suitcase a tin of ham and took it out to the gardener's daughter. Refusing Rae's offer of help, Miss Beckwith went into the kitchen to assist her and the General followed Rae into the drawing-room and stood in front of a window—his eyes appeared to be on the scene before him, but Rae knew that he was looking at her covertly and struggling to interpret the greeting she had received from his nephew.

Before he could bring the conversation round to Richard, Judy burst into the room. The sight of Richard's car in the drive had informed her of his presence, and her first words to Rae plunged the General deeper into mystification.

"What did I tell you?" she said. "It worked! Where is the beast?"

"If you're referring to your brother," said the General, "he's upstairs with your mother, showing his friend to his room."

"Friend?" Judy swung round to Rae. "What friend?"

"The one we met—Edward."

"Him! What in Christmas," demanded Judy angrily, "did he want to bring *him* down for?"

Men and Angels

"He's brought him down for the week-end," said the General. "He looks a harmless enough young man."

"Of course he's harmless," said Judy irritably. "That's what's wrong with him. Who's going to look after *him*, I'd like to know?"

"Since he's Richard's guest," said the General, "I've no doubt Richard will—what's his name, by the way?"

"Name? Oh—Peake, or something," said Judy. "Rae, did Richard say anything?"

A blush, which did not escape the General, overspread Rae's cheeks.

"No, nothing in particular," she said.

The door opened to admit Richard and his friend, and Judy gave her brother a cold glance.

"London too warm?" she enquired.

"By far," said Richard with his usual lazy ease. "How's the School of Art? Oh, by the way—you know Edward, don't you?"

"I've met him, yes. How d'you do," said Judy, making an effort.

Edward, gazing at her adoringly, was understood to say that he was very well. He was about to add a word or two about the weather, but having got as far as pretty warm, had to be rescued by the General.

"The heat's too sudden," he remarked. "It's drying everything up. Richard, have you asked Mr. Peake whether he'd care for a drink?"

"Mr.—oh, Edward! No thanks, sir, we had a couple on the way down. Pity they've built round that old pub."

"The 'Cock and Bull'? Yes, great pity," said the General. "You'll see a lot of changes for the worse, I'm afraid. They're pulling down all those lovely old thatched cottages near Marefield. Ah! here you are, my dear."

"Shall we go in to dinner now?" said Lady Ashton from the door. "Blanche is in the dining-room."

The men were left to their port after dinner, and the ladies pursued a stately way back to the drawing-room. Miss Beckwith got out her patience cards, Lady Ashton opened her cookery books and turned the pages placidly. Only Rae and Judy were restless.

Judy was not looking forward to the week-end. Her first sense of triumph had passed, and she now realised that it was impossible to find out what had brought Richard home; she could mention the party, but was unwilling to risk making him suspicious, and she was beginning to realise that she would never learn more than she knew now. Her scheme had brought about the desired result: Richard was here, but if she wanted matters between him and Rae to advance, she must leave them together—and if she left them together she would have Edward on her hands. He was a guest in her home, and she would be expected to treat him with courtesy. Her only escape lay in avoidance, but this week-end there could be no escape; Richard would drive Rae about, and she would be, she reflected moodily, stuck with Edward.

Miss Beckwith saw with pleasure that the dark man who had so puzzled her for the past three nights was now identified. The fair woman had pointed to Rae, but there was no accounting for the persistence with which the dark man had turned up again and again. Now, after that little scene in the hall, all was clear. She placed the two cards together and looked at them speculatively.

Lady Ashton was also speculating, and her usual placidity was a little ruffled; she had distinctly noticed Richard kissing Miss Mansfield in the hall, and she wondered why she had never connected the two in her mind before. The girl was very pretty, and had a gentle manner that one didn't often see nowadays; she and Judy were close friends, and it was natural that Judy should try to bring them together. Why Richard had let the girl spend nearly a week here without him was something his mother found it difficult to understand; perhaps she could have a word or two with Judy later.

"What," she asked, looking up, "is the name of that quiet young man?"

"Who?" Judy looked up with a start. "Oh—him. Deane, or something. Came home on the boat with Richard. I can't understand why somebody didn't push him overboard on the way."

"He seems charming, Judy."

"Oh, Mother, he's *terrible*! He's practically inarticulate!"

"That's only shyness, dear," put in Miss Beckwith.

"That's just it—he's too *old* to be shy. People have to learn how to get over all that."

"He'll get over it, I expect," said Lady Ashton.

"Well, he should stay away from people till he does," said Judy. "Why should I have to bring him out? I'm not a charm school, am I? Before this week-end's over he'll—"

She stopped as the door opened to admit the three men, Lady Ashton lifted the cookery books to make room for her son, but Richard shook his head.

"No, Mother darling," he said. "This is the Silence room and Edward's a terror—talks his head off. I'm going to take him and the girls upstairs to the old playroom. Come on, Rae."

He held out a hand, and Rae found that she had risen and put her own into it. Richard led her out of the room with a backward glance at Judy and Edward.

"Come on, you two."

The four went upstairs to the big playroom which Rae had seen on her arrival. Richard kicked aside the rugs issuing orders as he did so.

"Go and get my wireless out of my bedroom, Judy. Edward, shove those chairs back—we're going to dance."

There was a little difficulty in finding dance music; the wireless offered, in turn, a talk on the Development of Plastics, a lady singing English Folk Songs, and an endless series of voices talking at great speed in foreign tongues.

"Listen to that, said Richard, pausing in his knob-turning. "Doesn't he sound cross! "

"Oh, go on—*music,*" said Judy. "There—stop. No go back a bit—that's it. That's nice."

She watched Richard take Rae into his arms, waited for Edward's hesitating approach and was thankful to find that his feet worked a great deal better than his tongue. She was the more thankful as it became obvious that there was to be no changing of partners. She watched Richard open a window and lead Rae to the balcony. It was still light, and the air which came in was cool and pleasant. Richard nodded towards the lovely scene.

"Nice country," he said. "Like it?"

"Yes," said Rae.

"I thought you would. What have you been doing all the week?"

"What have you?" asked Rae, to her own surprise.

"Making love to Rosanna," said Richard without the slightest hesitation. "D'you mind?"

"No, I don't mind," said Rae quietly. "All I mind is the fact that you made love to me first."

"That's good," said Richard. "I shouldn't have liked it if you'd taken it too calmly. Can you remember where we left off?"

"No," said Rae. "But we did leave off."

"When I was a little shaver," said Richard, putting up a

hand and gently pushing her hair off her face, "I used to put the nicest bit of my food into the middle of the plate—like that, see?" He indicated a spot on the balustrade. "Then I used to put all the other food round the titbit and eat it—and every now and then I'd go back and have a nibble off the titbit. You follow me, I trust?"

"Perfectly," said Rae. "What happened if you came back to the titbit and it wasn't there?"

"Wasn't there?"

"Supposing it had moved?"

"That would have been awkward," admitted Richard, "but unlikely. All the things that moved were taken out of our food before we got it."

"I see. Why aren't we dancing?" asked Rae.

"Because we're enjoying this lovely June evening—did you mind being kissed in the hall?"

"I thought it was a little unnecessary. Your mother—"

"That's the point," said Richard. "In the eyes of the family, we're linked for ever."

"Are we?—That's a nice tune they're playing."

"Yes, isn't it? Did you miss me?"

Rae stared into the distance, a little frown on her brow. "A little at first," she answered slowly. "Then I don't think I did."

"And was Judy what might be called pettish when I didn't turn up?"

"Quite pettish. She thought I'd be bored if you weren't

Men and Angels

here, but I wasn't."

"Then you must have what are called inner resources. Home's home, but it isn't where you come when you want to be entertained. But speaking of actresses, we—"

"Were we?"

"I imagined we were. You must remember that I've come home after a long, long exile in places where one yearns in vain for the sight of an English face and the touch of an English skin and—"

"Judy says there are lots of English girls in Nairobi."

"Don't get in a fellow's way when he's taking off. I was going to tell you that when the exile goes back to his—his exile, as it were, he has to give his friends a long and colourful account of all the dashing adventures he's had. It's no use telling them about the shows he's seen—he's got to reel off the names of all the actresses he's taken out to dinner and—"

"You mean Rosanna's only the first?"

"By a long chalk. I've got to work up from there, higher and higher, until I'm photographed with the latest star in the latest night club. 'Our picture shows Miss Ravisha Starr with the well-known and popular Mr. Richard Ashton.' That goes over big when you get back."

"To your exile—or to your titbit?"

"Exile, naturally. I see you're picking up the idea. Take a camel," he invited. "He goes for long, dreary, dusty, thirsty weeks without a drop—so when he turns up at an oasis he gets

155

down to it and makes up for lost time. He drinks his fill. And so does the exile. After a surfeit of dusky complexions, he catches up on the world-renowned English kind."

"Is Edward catching up too?"

"He's trying. He was pretty fluent on the boat—he had his plans all laid. A stage star on Monday, screen star on Tuesday, tennis star on Wednesday, society belle on Thursday"—Richard ticked them off earnestly on his fingers— "let me see, skating star on Friday and a charming little model for the weekend."

"How's he doing?" asked Rae calmly,

"Badly. He's got everything but the patter, and that eludes him. That's why I hoped Judy'd take him in hand— if there's a girl that doesn't worry about pauses in the conversation, it's Judy. You can see how well he dances— but the poor mutt can't talk. He just—could I say he just mutters?"

"I wouldn't," advised Rae. "Come in and see if you can dance too."

Richard, throwing away his cigarette, followed her inside. He drew the curtains behind him and switched on the lights. The music to which they were dancing gave way to a Glee Club, and they turned the knob until they found something more rhythmic.

At ten o'clock, the General opened the door and appeared anxious to say something. Judy turned down the music.

"I looked in to speak about church on Sunday," said the

Men and Angels

General. "The orders for the cars have to be given tomorrow morning, and I don't suppose any of you will be down very early. How are we going to arrange it, Richard?"

Visitors to Thorpe Lodge were not asked whether they wished to go to church; they were merely asked which church they would attend. As the churches lay in different directions, cars had to be ordered accordingly. Richard began to count.

"You and Mother and Miss Beckwith—does the car hold anymore?"

"Not comfortably," said the General, who had no wish to sit on the little seat. "Will Judy's car—"

"No," said Judy.

"I suppose I can take four if we're all going the same way," said Richard. "Where d'you go, Rae? C. of E. four miles; R.C. six miles. Presbyterian six—"

"Six and a half," said the General.

"—and Baptist, Congregational, Seventh-day Adventist, Christadelphians, Friends and the Synagogue completely out of reach—well?"

"Church of England, please."

"And Judy the same, unless she's decanted since I was last home," said Richard. "Edward?"

"I imagine decanted isn't quite the word you want," said the General. "Or perhaps it was a joke."

"Thank you, sir. Edward?"

Edward was understood to say that he would go wherever

it gave the least trouble.

"Then that's fixed," said Richard. "You go as usual with Mother and Miss Beckwith, sir; I take these three in my export mod."

"That's all right, then," said the General. "You'll put the lights out, won't you, Richard?"

"What a good idea! I'll do it the moment you've gone, sir." Richard closed the door behind the General and switched out all the lights. "Though I must say," he remarked with his lips against Rae's in the darkness "it's a surprising suggestion to come from an old-fashioned old boy like Uncle Bertram."

Chapter Eleven

Early next morning it became obvious that Judy's apprehensions were well founded: she was to be left to Edward. At eight o'clock there was a knock on Rae's door, and it opened to reveal Richard on the threshold, fully dressed holding her tray.

"Good morning, good morning," he said heartily, entering. "You like the tray in bed with you, or on a table beside you?"

"Go away," said Rae.

"Don't be silly—I've brought in your breakfast. Is this all you eat?"

Rae, checking an impulse to say that it was all she was given to eat, merely nodded.

"You can't build yourself up on toast," said Richard. "Look at me," he invited, sitting on the edge of her bed and thumping his chest. "Porridge, egg and tomato, toast and marm—and three cups of nice hot coffee."

"Did you make your mother go down and make all that?"

"Mother? Good Lord, no! I took the gardener's daughter

aside and whispered my wants into her ear, that's all."

"Go away, please," said Rae.

"Why aren't you up?" demanded Richard. "I made sure you'd be up with the lark—I looked out of my window expecting to see you tripping among the flower-beds, getting some fresh air. Go on—eat that and get up. We're going out —you and I and a nice packed lunch."

"What about Judy?"

"Judy? Did I come down here to take Judy around? Besides, what'll Edward do?"

"Judy's done so much driving lately. Can't you—"

"—take them along? No. She's got a good strong pair of feet and so's Edward." He rose and looked down at her. "I'll give you thirty minutes. Meet you in the stable yard. I'll go and get the car out."

Just over half an hour later, they left the house and sped smoothly along a sunlit road. By noon they were seated on the car cushions on a hillside, and Richard was spreading out the contents of the lunch basket.

"Cold chicken, tinned ham, hard-boiled eggs and potatoes in their jackets—not bad. There was a nice bit of cold pie, but I left it for Uncle Bertram—he likes his bit of cold pie, does Uncle. There you are—there's your share."

"It looks nice," said Rae.,

"Of course it looks nice. I told that girl to make it look nice. You've got to let people know what you want, and then you get it. Leave them to themselves, and you'll find yourself landed with fish-paste sandwiches or something of the kind—what did they give you when you went out? I bet it was fish paste—was it?"

"It was all right," said Rae. "I didn't eat it I mean, I got lunch at the farm."

"But you didn't take the fish paste back and throw it at them?" Richard sighed. "You'll never do. I suppose Miss Beckwith said fish paste and you murmured a gentle thanks."

"Why not?"

"Because it's dishonest. And it's moral cowardice. People like you, my angelic little Rae, make the excuse that they don't like to give trouble—but it's only an excuse. What they don't like is speaking up, brave and bold, and airing their preferences. You're easy money for anybody who wants to get out of doing something for you. 'I hope you'll let me know what you want,' they say—but you don't, and so you get what they want."

"Well, that saves trouble, doesn't it?"

"It might; but if you look closely, you'll find that you get a good deal of the second best. Don't you mind that?"

"No."

"I don't believe you do," said Richard slowly. "Nobody could call you the pushing sort, could they? No wonder you and Judy get on. What are you going to do when you fall in love—let him walk over you?"

"If he was the walking-over sort, I wouldn't like him."

"Empty words. Those heavily shod types always go straight for the gentle little yous—speaking of empty, that basket's still quite full. If you'll pour out the coffee, I'll count out the tarts." Having counted them out in the ratio of three to one, Richard helped himself to the lion's share and lay back contentedly looking up at the blue sky.

"Lovely day, lovely Rae," he chanted. "Why d'you spell your name with an e? It's short for Raymonde, isn't it? It ought to be R-a-y, isn't that right?"

Rae took so long to answer that Richard rolled over and glanced at her curiously. At the look on her face he propped himself up on an elbow and repeated his question.

"Isn't it Raymonde?"

Rae's cheeks became pink.

"Well, no," she said. "It—well, it isn't."

"Then what is it? Something frightful?"

"Well, yes—it is, rather. It's—it's Raedburh."

"It's *what*!"

"Raedburh." Rae spelt it out slowly.

"Where on earth did your parents get that one?" enquired Richard in astonishment. "And what does it mean?"

"It doesn't mean anything, as far as I know," said Rae. "It's the name of a queen."

"You were a queen, were you?"

Rae nodded.

"Yes. I was the first Queen of the English. My husband was somebody called Egbert and—"

"Egbert!"

"Yes, I'm afraid so. He was the son of the King of Kent, and he was driven into exile to the court of Charlemagne."

"Did you go into exile with him?"

"It doesn't say. Egbert came back and subjugated West Wales, beat the King of Marcia, annexed Kent and then became the first King of the English. They called him Rex Anglorum."

"That makes you Regina Anglorum. Regina Anglorum—and there you sit in a mended coat and—"

"The Duchess tore it."

"Would she have torn it if she'd realised who you were. No! That's a further proof of the way you let people walk all over you—but we won't dwell on that. Did you have any children?"

"I had a son called Ethelwulf."

"The first English wolf. What happened to him?"

"He married somebody called Osburgha, and she had four sons—one of them was Alfred the Great."

"Alfred the Great? You mean the fellow who let the cakes go to charcoal?"

"Yes."

"Great Scott!" said Richard, sitting up and regarding her with awe. "You mean you're Alfred the Great's grandmother?"

"I'm the grandmother of four Kings," said Rae with pardonable pride. "Ethel*bald,* Ethel—"

"Yes, yes, yes," said Richard hastily. "But where did your parents find a name like Raedburh?"

"My father was an historian," explained Rae. "He was drawing up a chart of the Saxon Kings when I was born."

"Then you were damn lucky to get off with Raedburh. I'm not strong on Saxon history, but if my memory isn't at fault, there were girls running about at that time with names like Estrith and Gytha and Aelflaed and Aethelbarh. You were comparatively lucky—you'd think parents could be suppressed, but they go on tying the most humiliating labels on to their helpless infants. Even Judy didn't get off scot-free."

"I know. That's why I first liked her—I heard her complaining that she'd been called Julienne, like a soup and it—"

"—drew you to her. I've nothing to draw you with—I'm merely Richard." He lay back once more and closed his eyes. "High up on a hill, all alone with Alfred the Great's grandmother," he murmured. "Be still, my heart."

There was long silence. Richard broke it by turning to her and speaking a little abruptly.

You know," he said, "you're very sweet."

He had said it before, but he had never said it in quite this way. Rae, looking at him, saw that all trace of his normal sardonic, teasing manner had left him; the eyes that looked into hers were serious, brooding, a little puzzled, somewhat at a loss, Rae looked back at him without speaking and after a while, he went on in the same quiet manner.

"We met," he said, "at rather a disadvantage. Judy can talk fluently enough, but her letters don't convey anything that she wants to convey. They didn't, for example, prepare me for you."

"Judy's sweet, but I always hoped she wouldn't—"

"—throw us at one another. Being Judy, she did. You sounded just the girl to make a man's leave pass quickly and pleasantly. She said that you were lovely to look at, quiet to have around, and of a meek and retiring disposition. When I met you, I found that only the first two were correct; you were lovely to look at, and you didn't cause any noticeable disturbance—but you weren't the somewhat self-effacing type she'd labelled you."

"You like the self-effacing type?" enquired Rae.

"No. That's why I was unprepared. And thats why I was caught. I went out to have a nice evening, and I ended up by forgetting about the evening and thinking about you. I went on thinking about you. I went on until you gave me a jolt by throwing me over for your aunts—and the jolt was such a severe one that I came to the conclusion I'd done a great deal too much thinking about one particular girl. When you come home on leave, I told myself, you don't concentrate on one special girl, however beautiful; you spread yourself out and take in all the lovely girls you can induce to go out with you—that sounds a reasonable way of spending a leave, doesn't it?"

"Very reasonable," agreed Rae.

"So I decided to stop concentrating. And thats why I went to see your friend Rosanna."

"She isn't my—"

"Your old schoolmate, Rosanna. She was very kind to me, and she understood exactly how leaves should be spent. But I found that I went on thinking about one girl—round and round in circles. And it wasn't about Rosanna I was thinking. It was about you."

There seemed nothing to say to this, and Rae remained silent. Richard appeared to need no answer; he lay brooding, his eyes gazing upward at the blue sky. She examined her own feelings, and found them difficult to define. He was telling her that he loved her, and he sounded serious, but she had gone too fast once, and she was never again going to allow herself to rush precipitantly into misery and regret. She had imagined that she understood him, and he had acted in a manner that she had found incomprehensible; he had explained his actions to his own satisfaction, but he had left out of his account any possibility that she was entitled to a share of his consideration. He appeared to have spent a great deal of time dwelling upon his own feelings, but had wasted little thought on hers; he had not touched upon her reactions at arriving and finding that he was amusing himself elsewhere. She had no wish to remind him, but she felt something of her resentment returning. Watching her changing expressions, Richard, after a while, smiled.

"Another thing Judy didn't tell me," he said.

"What?"

"That you have a base and ungenerous nature, and harbour grudges."

She laughed a little as she denied it.

"I haven't, and I don't," she said.

"But you'll admit," said Richard, "that things aren't the same—between you and me—as they were in London?"

"They're not quite the same," said Rae slowly.

Richard got to his feet and pulled her to hers. His manner was once again light and bantering.

"They will be again," he promised. "I only need time—and tea."

They had tea at an inn deep in the woods, and drove home slowly, Richard holding her hand in his favourite position under his on the wheel. He drove across the cobbled stable-yard and into the garage.

"Tomorrow?" he said.

"Tomorrow's Sunday—church."

"Well, after church. We'll have lunch at home and then go out—yes?"

"Yes," said Rae.

He left her at the end of her corridor, and she walked slowly to her room and closed the door. It opened again almost immediately, and Judy came in, her expression one of resigned boredom.

"Nice day?" she asked.

"Very nice. I'm afraid," said Rae regretfully, "that this isn't turning out much of a week-end for you."

"It would have been all right," said Judy, "if Richard hadn't brought that inarticulate idiot and left me to deal with him. You told me not to insult people and—honestly, Rae, I'm trying, but it comes hard. This Edward mumbles something, and when you've asked him politely, twice, to repeat it, it turns out to be some gem like 'Nice country you've got here,' or 'Peaceful spot, this,' or 'Decent cattle. Anybody of his age—he's twenty-five—I asked him; anybody of his age who can't make up his mind what to say and how to say it, ought to stay at home until he can."

"He's all right when he's talking to me," said Rae. "I think that every time he looks at you, he gets tongue-tied."

"That's what I'm saying," said Judy. "He ought to go away and talk to somebody else. I'm tired of coaxing all his speeches out of him like a diction mistress—when's he going home?"

"Richard's going to drive him into Sheafton Abbott on Monday morning and put him on the train."

"Not on," implored Judy. "Under."

Chapter Twelve

On Sunday afternoon, it was Edward who drove the export model, Judy by his side; Richard and Rae went for a long, leisurely walk down to the village. Judy returned looking unhappy, but resigned; they had driven, she told Rae, to see an aunt of Edward's, who lived near Allbrook.

"What was she like?" asked Rae.

"Just like him—to look at. Like a depressed spaniel, but at any rate she could talk. She's his only relation—mother dead, father dead, everybody dead—only this aunt left. She mistook me for his girl-friend and showed me pictures of him in rompers—if I'd had any feeling for him before, that would've killed it."

"I would have thought he would have been a sweet little boy," said Rae reflectively. "Round pink face with a lost expression."

"D'you know what she said, Rae?—She said he was wonderful at telling children stories. Him!"

"Well, perhaps he isn't shy with children."

"Perhaps," said Judy indifferently. "Thank goodness tomorrow'll see the end of him. Richard's taking him in to catch the morning train."

Rae was glad to hear it; she had an appointment to keep, and she was anxious to keep it without Richard. She had promised to go swimming, and she wanted to go without having to answer the questions which Richard would undoubtedly ask.

Judy drove away early on Monday morning; some time later, Edward sought Rae out in the garden.

"I'm just off," he said, in his soft voice.

"Oh, are you? Good-bye, Edward. I hope you'll come and see us when we're back in Town."

"I'd like to, awfully. Thanks. Thanks awfully—I suppose I'd better say a word to the General before I go, hadn't I? Do you happen to know where he is?"

"He s in the greenhouse—at least, he was a few moments ago."

"Well, thanks. Thanks awfully. I'll go and find him."

Rae watched him go, and found herself, for the first time, somewhat in agreement with Judy's views. People ought to—she paused to return Edward's wave—people should try to overcome shyness. Edward was—in his mournful way— good-looking. He would be a welcome member of any society if only he could—Rae fell back on Judy's expression—string two words together. As it was...

She heard Richard's voice beside her.

"It's pretty hot, isn't it? You're looking nice and cool—

Men and Angels

and very thoughtful. What were you brooding on?"

"Edward. Perhaps Judy's right and he ought to shut himself up somewhere and shout out loud until he gets used to the sound of his own voice."

"I don't agree," said Richard. "There're far too many voices shouting in the world. The whole planet's one vast yap yap yap. People talk all the time, mostly about nothing. We want more Edwards."

"But if he talked more—or at any rate, talked more fluently, then people would be able to get to know him better."

"There's nothing wrong with Edward. He's a pretty smart chap, when you come to know him. He plays good tennis, good golf, good bridge, and he holds down a good job. I'm very fond of Edward. You girls ought to look beyond obvious charms like mine and explore the more subtle ones of the Edwards. Here he comes—oh, I'll be out to lunch—will you tell Mother? Edward's giving me lunch."

"Edward? But he's—he's going back to—"

"To Town? No, he isn't—he's changed his mind. Haven't you, Neddy my boy?"

"Yes."

"But you said good-bye!"

"Well, I'm going," explained Edward, "but I'm not going to London. I'm—as a matter of fact, I'm putting up at the—at the inn at Allbrook. It's—it's a bit hot for London."

"Allbrook!" Rae hoped that there was more surprise than

dismay in her exclamation, but in her mind was Judy's face of relief when she had spoken of Edward's departure. And now he was to be almost next door to her....

"How long are you staying there?" she asked.

"Well, I don't know. It rather depends on—on how things go, as it were," said Edward. "Won't you drive over and have lunch with us?"

"No, thank you," said Rae. "I'm—well, no, thank you, all the same."

She walked with them to the car and stood watching it out of sight. She went slowly back and saw the General coming across the lawn.

"They've gone, have they?"

"Yes."

"It's going to be hot—a pity, as I've got to walk round and see one or two things this afternoon. Don't fancy it in this heat. What do you plan to do with yourself, eh?"

"I'm going to—well, I'm seeing the people at the farm—I promised the boys."

"Ah yes. Well, you'll get some shade if you—" He stopped abruptly, staring at the sweep of gravel in front of the house. Rae, turning, saw to her surprise a bath chair standing on the drive; a familiar figure was climbing stiffly out of it. The General muttering something unintelligible under his breath, took a step forward to greet her.

The Duchess came towards them, and Rae saw that she

was extremely short—less than five feet—and stout. She was dressed for the heat-wave—her coat and skirt were of shantung, her stockings of grey silk, and her shoes a pair of pale grey kid of a kind so old-fashioned that Rae found it difficult to keep her eyes off them.

The Duchess showed no reciprocal interest; she approached with firm strides, surprisingly long in so squat a figure, and stopped before the General.

"Ah, General! Good morning."

"How d'you do, Duchess?" The General's greeting, though polite, was not cordial. He stood looking down upon the caller, and Rae thought that he looked like a camel stooping down to identify a mound in the sand.

"Very hot, don't you find?" asked the Duchess, in her sharp accents. "Don't care for the heat, m'self. Your sister well, I hope?"

"Very well, thank you. Won't you—"

"Came round to see about a picture," said the Duchess. "Understand that that artist, what's his name—Aylmer Ferris—is doing a portrait of Lady Ashton. That so?"

"Yes," said the General. He turned towards Rae. "I don't think you've met—"

"Yes, I have. Silly gel. Sees a vehicle approaching, and puts herself immediately in front of it. Never saw anything so dangerous—might have upset the whole thing and flung me into the hedge."

She glared at Rae, obviously waiting for an apology but Rae, summoning her fortitude, kept her lips closed: The Duchess, with a contemptuous toss of the polo topee, resumed her conversation with the General.

"I'm by way of giving an exhibition—I've got all those students from the Art School coming up to the Castle on Friday week, bringing their stuff with them. Be a good thing, I thought, to include this picture that Ferris is doing of your sister—no objection to that, I suppose?"

"You must ask my—"

"I'll only keep it a day, and I'll fetch it myself—I've got to use the car to collect the stuff from Allbrook, so it won't be out of my way. Friday morning, and tell your sister to take every care, naturally."

"Perhaps," began the General, "you d better—"

"Come up yourself, if you like, in the afternoon, I'm throwing the place open, but I'm not going to let 'em in without charging an entrance fee, naturally."

"Naturally." The General's word fell and froze, like an icicle.

"Going now. Y'r garden's looking as brown as mine," said the Duchess. "These dry spells don't do anything any good—There's a nice property beyond Marefield coming on the market—wouldn't interest you, I suppose?"

"I'm afraid not."

The Duchess gave what Rae, in anybody else, would have

called a sniff.

"Can't understand why you ever gave up an establishment of your own to come and live with a couple of women. Always told me it was a temporary thing, and you're still here. You'd be much better up at Marefield, and you'd get some good rough shooting. I never could understand why people let servants drive 'em out of their houses. Servants can be had, and kept, if you know how to set about it. Naturally, if you're going to give 'em the best rooms and the best china, and pay 'em enormous wages to go out and enjoy themselves, you've only yourself to blame when they assume you're working for them."

"The problem—"

"No problem at all. People like ourselves have got to have service, and good service. I've got it, haven't I? And do I pander? Certainly not. Facts are facts and people have to face 'em. 'Look here,' I say to them, 'God made me a Duchess, God only knows why, and He made you a footman and there it is; it's no use your railing against the fact—I don't suppose you enjoy it any more than I do, but you just go away and make up your mind to be a competent footman, and I'll run my end of it as well as I can.' That's what I say, and the thing becomes quite clear. D'you think that servants don't know when you make yourself uncomfortable on their account?—and do they thank you for it? No. You take my advice, General—you take that place up at Marefield and keep up an establishment. The Government tried to tax me out and the servants tried to drive me out, and I'm still there. Let 'em go on trying—if you want to talk to my Agent about that property, you know where to find him. Good-bye; Friday morning. Tell Lady Ashton sorry, can't stop to say 'How do'. Good-bye. Tell that silly gel to look where she's going."

Throughout this harangue, the General had stood looking down at a point in the air just above the polo topee The stream ending, he bowed, handed the Duchess into her chair, and stood with Rae watching her disappearing round the bend.

"A charming woman," he remarked with heavy sarcasm.

"Yes," murmured Rae. "Delightful."

"One can do nothing," explained the General, "but listen."

"I know." Rae's voice was soft and sympathetic. "It's really so silly, because—well, you're twice her size, and you could pick her up so easily and drop her over the wall but because she's half your size, and a woman—"

"Ha-ha quite so," said the General, completely restored by the knowledge that someone was so wholly on his side.

"I could pick her up ha-ha-ha—and can't you just see the picture, ha-ha!—But, by Jove, that reminds me—I'd better go indoors and say something to Lady Ashton about it."

"Oh, and please—would you tell her that Richard will be out to lunch?"

"Where's he lunching?" asked the General.

"With Edward—Edward's going to stay at the inn at Allbrook."

"Inn at Allbrook? That's where all those Art students are, isn't it? And Judy. I heard Judy say she was glad to get rid of that feller—how can she be rid of him if he's going to be in her pocket all through the week?"

"He's—he's got an aunt near there," said Rae.

"Well, if he's got an aunt, can't he go and stay with her. What's he doing—running after Judy?"

"Well, I don't really know. It seems rather a waste of his time, in a way. Judy doesn't—"

"Well, she might do worse," put in the General unexpectedly. "Don't know a thing about the feller except that he doesn't talk. And if Judy gets hold of a feller who *does*, I don't know where he'd fit in what he had to say."

He went inside, looking thoughtful, and Rae was left to ponder on his words. She came to the conclusion that Edward must be given credit for exceptional tenacity; no man had ever received less encouragement. Richard had said he was good at a great many things; Rae found herself hoping that he was also a good loser.

She set off after lunch and, with an unfamiliar feeling of duplicity, turned in the direction of the farm and walked for some distance before branching off towards the swimming-pool. She reached it, to find the boys out of sight and Bianca sitting on the bank pulling off her dungarees.

"I'm going to thwim," she shouted.

"Well, wait till I get in," said Rae, taking her suit from the bush on which the boys had placed it. "Wait till I come, and I'll teach you how to stay on top."

She swam on her back, drawing Bianca's small, kicking figure through the water, while Hugh and Alan gave a diving display which had in it more splash than skill.

"Was that one better, Rae?" shouted Alan, surfacing after a particularly unsuccessful attempt at a standing swallow.

"No it wasn't; it was worse—your feet were miles apart."

"Well, watch this one," said Alan, scrambling out and getting into position. "Are you looking? I'll do a—" He broke off abruptly and straightened slowly, gazing at his brother.

"What's up?" asked Hugh.

"Did you hear anything?"

"Hear—no, I didn't."

"Well, I'm sure I did. Listen. Oh, shut up, Bi-an-KER."

Rae put a hand softly on the tiny mouth, and everybody waited, listening intently. In a few moments there was the unmistakable sound of a long-drawn-out whistle; before it had died away, both boys were on the bank and reaching for Bianca.

"Hand her up, Rae—come on, Bi-an-KER—quick."

"Wheres the other towel?" asked Hugh. "Oh there, Quick, throw it across, Rae. Now, all into those bushes—hurry!"

He parted a thick mass of foliage, and Rae, with some difficulty, pushed her way through and pulled Bianca behind her. She found that they had entered a little clearing in which they could sit comfortably, unobserved except by anybody standing close to the bushes and looking down at them. They arranged themselves and their clothes silently; Bianca, to whom the procedure was new, looked on in wide- eyed curiosity.

"Are we going to thwim and—"

Hugh put a hand over her mouth and glared at her fiercely.

"Quiet!" he hissed. "Don't you say one single word—don't you even breathe, d'you understand? There's someone coming who'll swallow you up whole if he hears you—understand?"

Bianca s eyes indicated that she understood, but was not unduly impressed. Hugh released her, not entirely satisfied, and stood up to scan the approaches. The others waited in silence.

"Down," whispered the sentry suddenly. "He's coming. Old Ginger-whiskers."

A breathless hush fell; Bianca stared at her brothers, and they stared back, ready to stifle any sound issuing from her lips. For some moments she remained unmoved, but the tension soon communicated itself to her, and as the sound of the approaching enemy was heard, she put up a hand and clutched her nose tightly. Rae looked at her with dismay, watching her face grow pinker, and wondered whether she would be able to hold out until the footsteps went by.

There was a steady tramp, uncomfortably close and then the footsteps became fainter. Alan raised himself slightly and peered out.

"He's going," he reported. "Give him ten minutes and then he won't hear us. Bi-an-KER, what're you doing holding your nose?"

Bianca, now purple, released her nose and drew several gasping breaths.

"I didn't breathe," she announced triumphantly.

"Well you can breathe now," said Rae. She stretched her cramped legs, but found herself still with a strange sense of tension. Looking at the boys, she saw to her surprise that they were far from easy; they wore anxious frowns, and were still unwilling to go into the open.

"He's gone, hasn't he?" asked Rae.

"Yes" Alan sounded unconvinced. I suppose we'd better go out now. I can't see old Ginger-whiskers."

"Old Ginger-whiskers," said a frosty voice above them, "is entirely out of sight."

Rae felt all her strength dram out of her. She saw the boys' faces, white and upturned. Only Bianca looked up at the speaker with unabashed interest.

"Come on out, all of you," came a crisp order.

The party made a crouching and undignified reappearance and stood upright. Rae, rising to her feet, stared into the cold eyes of Richard Ashton.

"Well," he said slowly, "this is a fine—a very fine thing."

Alan had recovered a little of his poise.

"If we are trespassing, then so are you, because this belongs to—"

"It belongs to my mother. Did she give you permission to come here?"

"Your mother? But I thought," said Hugh in surprise, "that old—that it belonged—I mean, it was General Fitzroy who put up all those gates and padlocks and everything."

"And you ignored the hint?"

"It wasn't your fault," said Hugh indignantly. "It was us. We—"

"Yes it was us," said Allen. "We swam all last year before you were here, and—"

"I did too. I did thwim," shouted Bianca triumphantly.

"Oh pipe down." ordered Hugh.

"It was a pretty sight," said Richard, addressing Rae, "to see you creeping into bushes and—"

"I didn't breathe!" yelled Bianca.

"Quiet!" ordered Richard. "I'm talking. What was the matter with asking permission?" he went on. "If you'd told the General you wanted a swim, he'd—"

"She couldn't," pointed out Alan. "Not without giving us away. And she didn't know we weren't allowed to come. —we didn't tell her."

"I see. She thought she was just crawling into the bushes for fun—is that it?"

"There's not much point in talking about it, is there?"

asked Rae. "What are you going to do?"

"Tell my uncle," said Richard without hesitation.

There was silence. Hugh and Alan appeared to be weighing up the situation.

"I suppose you've really got to tell him, now you've seen us," agreed Hugh reasonably, "but we're only here for another week, about—couldn't you—?"

"No, I couldn't."

"Yes, you could," said Rae with surprising firmness. "You needn't say anything, and if you don't, I'll see that the boys ask your uncle—before they go away next week—for permission to swim in the summer."

"Crumbs!" said Alan. "He'll kick us out."

"It doesn't matter; you've got to ask him," said Rae.

"But it isn't even his—it's Lady Ashton's—he said so. Can't we ask her?"

"She'd tell you to go and ask the General," said Richard. "Do you promise, or don't you?"

"Suppose so," said Hugh gloomily.

"And next time you peer out of a hiding-place, peer all around you. You're a rotten Scout, if you're a Scout at all. I saw the whole thing, standing in the open, and you never no much as glanced in my direction. Is that the way to trespass?"

"We didn't expect you," said Rae.

"Well, you—and I mean you—should have expected me. You said you were going to the farm, and I walked all the ruddy way there, only to find that there wasn't, and hadn't been, any sign of you. So after prowling over the country-side, I caught sight of Uncle B., also on the prowl, and decided to follow him. And what do I find? You—practically a member of our household—aiding and abetting the—"

"I'm thwimming—look!" came a joyous cry from the water.

The three rescuers dived simultaneously, and Richard watched from the shore.

"Here you are, Richard—watch her," said Rae. "We're swimming to the other side."

"What you want," remarked Richard, bending down to haul out the small form, and thumping it vigorously on the back, "what you want is a coastguard service. There—that's most of the water out. Try the top layer—it isn't so wet," he advised.

"Did you thee me thwim?" enquired Bianca.

"Is that what you were doing? Well, you want a bit more practice. Look at Rae and the boys, now—now you watch, they're swimming to the other side. Now watch their legs see 'em? Out in, out in, like Alan—or you can make them go like flippers, like Rae's doing—see that? There they go—now they're having a race, see? No, you can't exactly join them until you've in a bit of—hey, where're you—hey! Whoa there, you what's-your-name. Whoa, I said. Come back, you lunatic infant, you. Come—oh, Christmas!"

"I'm thwimming," said Bianca, as she sank.

"Oh, God," moaned Richard, plunging after her. "So am I."

Chapter Thirteen

Rae was up early the next morning, and Richard found her in the garden, trying to persuade the sedate Bess to gambol.

"This dog won't unbend," she complained. "He can't be more than two, and he behaves like an old gentleman of sixty."

"She isn't more than two, and she behaves like an old lady of sixty," corrected Richard. "Did you hear me sneezing all through the night?"

"No."

"Well, I did. I think I've got pneumonia coming on, and I've ruined a pair of flannels and a brand-new sports coat. I wish I'd let that brat drown."

"I told you not to let her go. She's got the idea that the water'll keep her up, and"—Rae leaned against a tree and laughed—"oh! I wish you could have seen yourself."

"Glad to provide a spectacle at any time," said Richard. "What're you doing to-day? Let's drive."

"No, I can't. It's market day."

"Market day? You buy and sell?"

"The boys—Hugh and Alan—sell fruit and vegetables, so

I thought I'd go and help them. I went with them last week."

"Well, what time do we go?"

"Well, I don't think we do," said Rae slowly. There isn't much to interest you and—"

"I brought you down here to stave off long hours of loneliness, didn't I? Of course I'm coming."

They walked down to the village by a steep footpath. It was a direct route, but the going was difficult, and Richard expressed his gratification at finding Rae clinging to him for support.

"That's right—hang on. I'm here to rescue drowning damsels and support stumbling ones. Was that Judy who rang you up last night?"

"Yes."

"What did she say?"

"You know perfectly well what she said. And she thinks that you put the idea into Edward's head."

"Then she's wrong, because I didn't. Is he seeing much of her?"

"Not more than she can help. There isn't much to do there if he can't see Judy," remarked Rae. "What'll he do with his time?"

"Plenty. He's writing a book."

"A book!"

"Well no, not a book. But he's got a nice idea of adapting nursery rhymes to suit the needs of the modern nursery. He's bringing them up to date—stiffening them up."

"That's been done already—haven't they done it in, I forget which country—somewhere on the Continent?"

"Well, if they have, they've pinched his idea. Our idea—I thought of it too, but he's going to do the book, and see about the publishing before we go back."

"Isn't that rather quick work? I mean, won't a publisher take—"

"Not this time," said Richard. "We've got one taped. One of those big London johnnies."

"Do you know him?"

"Well no, we don't know him, but on the boat coming home there was a very fast piece—very fast piece indeed. Yes, very. What that girl went in for, you've no idea. Tck Tck Tck," Richard shook his head in disapprobation. "Most of us used to lock our cabin doors and shove our wardrobes up against them."

"Do ship's wardrobes—"

"These did—they were shoved by the strength of desperate men. Well, this piece turned out to be the daughter of this London publisher, so all we've got to do is go along and see the chap and bring up the little affair in the Red Sea, or the shocking bit of scandal just outside Suez—the fellow'll drop all his other commitments and concentrate on our book."

"I see. Is it finished?"

"Finished? No, not quite. We've got two quite good

rhymes done, though—we knocked 'em up between us over lunch yesterday. One's pretty good:

> *One, two*
>
> *Blood on my shoe;*
>
> *Three four Bash in the door;*
>
> *Five six*
>
> *Bash it with bricks;*
>
> *Seven eight*—let me see—*seven eight, seven eight*—oh!
>
> *Blood on his pate;*
>
> *Nine ten*
>
> *Hark at Big Ben.* There—how's that?"

"Terrible—it's all about blood."

"Well of course it is. It's for six-year-olds, and that's the most bloodthirsty age of all. Edward's got a good one going about *Who Killed Cock Robin?*—he's calling it *Blood in the Bird-bath.*"

"Well, I'll do without my autographed copy, thank you. Can't we get off this beastly road, Richard, Please? The stones are cutting right through my shoes."

"Grumble, grumble, grumble—some people are never satisfied," complained Richard. "I brought you down here to give you a sense of being alone with me—don't you like it?"

"Not in my feet."

"Well, we'll cut across and get on to the main road. This way."

The road became considerably worse for a few hundred yards, but at the end of them Richard swung Rae into his arms and put her over a low bush into the road beyond.

"There you are—nice and smooth. Come on."

Rae, instead of coming on, stood looking about her with a puzzled look.

"I've seen this corner before," she said slowly. "Oh *yes*! Richard, it's exactly where that—"

She stopped and leapt for the bush, but Richard had had the same saving thought one second earlier, and was occupying the only place of safety. The bath chair caught Rae a glancing blow, and the red face became purple.

"Silly gel," screamed the Duchess, disappearing round the next bend.

Rae sat in the hedge and looked at Richard, who was extricating himself from his refuge.

"How are you?" he enquired, looking himself over anxiously. "In one piece, I trust?"

"Yes, thank you," said Rae coldly. "It was kind of you to push me under the bath chair."

"Well, I thought you were making for that bush, and there wasn't room for two—and there wasn't time to explain, either. The instinct of self-preservation is a very strong one."

"I know—it pushed me. Is there a lawyer anywhere here?"

"Not one that would run the Duchess in for you, no."

"You mean, I'm just to be knocked down week after week

and—"

"You don't *move* quickly enough. Once you've been here a little while, you listen subconsciously for that whirring sound, and then you don't wait—you leap for the hedge. After all these years away, I still retain the instincts of my boyhood. I haven't heard that sound for—how many years? —and did you see me jump?"

"I did."

"Well, don't sit there—the market waits. Give me your hand."

He pulled Rae to her feet and dusted her, and the two walked down to the village. Hugh and Alan's sales were well advanced, and they greeted Rae with their usual friendliness, and Richard a shade less cordially.

"How's it going?" asked Richard.

"Oh—fine, thanks."

"Rae didn't want to bring me, so I came—I was sure you were up to something. Not giving short change I trust?"

"Of course they're not—don't be silly, please, Richard," said Rae.

"There's nothing silly about it. These two are criminal types. Any boys turned out of school and left kicking their heels are criminal types. Hurry along," he ordered. "I don't want to stand about with my pneumonia."

Hugh and Alan hurried along the next garden path, and Rae pushed the handcart slowly.

Men and Angels

"No connection between the glut of strawberries down here and the dearth at home, I suppose?" enquired Richard.

"Don't be silly." In spite of herself, Rae's cheeks became flushed, and Richard looked at her keenly.

"You're a fast worker," he said admiringly. "I leave you down here alone for less than a week, and you get tied up with a couple of—"

"They're nice, sensible—"

"—barrow boys. You stand in this market-place and hawk my uncle's fruit. You—"

"It isn't your uncle's. And the pool wasn't your uncle's—it's far more yours than your uncle's."

"That makes it a damn sight more serious. That garden's going to be mine one day—a quarter of it, anyhow. That means that one out of every four strawberries is mine. And yours, if I make up my mind to marry you when I've gone into the matter more thoroughly. It's odd how sentimental women are," he mused. "If you didn't like those two trainee criminals down there, you'd hand them over to justice at once—but they're nice and brown and leggy and appealing, so you aid and abet them—right?"

"I like them—yes."

"You won't make much of a mother," he commented. "It's rather shaken me. If I let you out of sight with our children, who's to know what you'll let them do?"

"The possibility's a bit remote, isn't it?" asked Rae.

191

"One never knows, with you," complained Richard. "I go to bed one night convinced I know you inside out, and the next day you have something in your manner—a shade—something I can't put my finger on, and then I find I have to go back and begin at the beginning. What makes you so elusive, Miss Mansfield?"

"Simple caution, Mr. Ashton. Your own manner is a little inconsistent, you know—Alan, will you take the cart now?"

Alan took the cart, and Rae began to walk slowly up the hill, with Richard by her side.

"Why did you bring Edward down here?" she asked.

"Edward? I didn't bring him down. He came with me, but that doesn't mean I brought him. He's in love; he finds out I'm coming down to be near his love, so he clings to me like a limpet and makes sure that he comes down with me.

How d'you think he's getting on?"

"With Judy?" Rae hesitated. "I think she finds him a little—inarticulate."

"For two reasons: the first is, of course, the effect she has on him. He tries to talk, looks at her, and forgets what he was going to say. But the second reason is a good one, too—she doesn't give him much chance to say anything. If he ever gets her at a moment when, for any reason, she's not discoursing, then perhaps he'll find his powers of speech which are quite considerable, when you get him at his best. Judy's not an easy girl to woo, would you say? She's got all my sourness and not half my tact. Instead of letting a fellow feel his way and take things slowly, she jumps on him for dragging, and drains all the courage out of him. I don't suppose Edward's the sort of fellow she thinks she'll marry; she's probably working on an ambitious project with a strong jaw and a silver tongue—but I think she'd do very well with Edward, if she ever had the sense to look at what he's got to offer. That's what I like so much about you—you let me do the talking. That's one thing. Then I like your looks, and your voice—when I hear it. And I like the way you order a drink and let me down it. I don't know very much of what you're thinking, but I'm beginning to learn something about your outlook on life—you don't, by the way, believe in free love for women?"

"I haven't—"

"I'm glad. I always think it's unbecoming in your sex and they've invariably told me afterwards that they wish they hadn't been so free. It's a broad topic—would you care for my views?"

"No, thank you."

"Some other time. Have you noticed that I'm keeping very close to the topic of love and marriage?"

"No," said Rae.

"You should have noticed. Any girl but you would have noticed and drawn her own conclusions." He stopped and leaning against a tree, looked at her with an unreadable expression. "I wonder," he said, "why I can't ever find out what you're thinking. At this moment, for instance—tell me Rae."

"I don't—"

"Please!"

"I was thinking," said Rae slowly, "how easily you—make your effects."

"What effects, please?"

"Any effects. You want to amuse somebody, so you amuse them; you want to tease them, and you can do it to perfection. You want something from them, so you set yourself to charm it out of them—all without any perceptible effort."

"And how, exactly, do I take that? Are you trying to say that nothing I do or say is—spontaneous?"

"I don't know about spontaneous. I only know that you, yourself, are rather difficult to read, because I don't think that you ever allow your real feelings to appear on the surface."

"I wonder," said Richard, "if any man ever had an advantage like mine and threw it away as lightly? Were we, or were we not, in love—both of us—when we were in London?"

"Who can say? We each liked what we saw, but how much did we see? When we saw a little more, we—loved a little less."

"I made one appalling mistake—I thought that what I felt for you wasn't—could be—the real thing. It was too swift and too smooth—I thought that we'd both been swept off our feet. I decided to make a test that's all."

"You gave yourself time to think. And you gave me time to think, too."

"And that was the mistake. But if I didn't consider your feelings then, I've thought about them ever since. I wonder about them all day and half the night. I try to find out what you're thinking, and how I stand with you, and I draw a blank—a whole series of blanks. I love you and you once loved me. If I hurt you, I'm sorry, but nobody as sweet and as gentle as you could allow—could—"

"I don't think you understand," said Rae gently. What happened was my fault—not yours. I should never have—"

"Rae," he broke in. "I love you. Will you marry me—"

There was a long silence.

"No, Richard," said Rae, at last. "No, I won't."

Chapter Fourteen

Throughout the following week, Richard proposed daily to Rae, who daily thanked him and declined. He made love to her with a warmth which she made no attempt to resist, she drove with him, walked or swam, danced night after night in the long, bare playroom. He outlined his plans for their marriage, his eyes on hers with a challenging gleam, and Rae listened with an answering gleam of amusement in her own.

They spent many hours at the farm. Mart accepted Richard with a casualness equal to his own; they approved greatly of one another. Rae sat on a kitchen chair, and Richard perched himself on the edge of the big table, performing efficiently such tasks as Mart gave him, and sampling each batch of cooking as it came out of the oven. Bianca made him a present of her favourite kitten. Mr Selwyn came in time to regard him as one of the permanent members of the staff. Reeny treated him with serene detachment, and marched him severely into meals. Only Hugh and Alan were depressed; they had lost in Rae a valued companion, and the date of their return to school loomed horrifyingly near.

At the Lodge, the affair—which Richard made no attempt

to hide—was watched with interest by the three older members of the household. The General, from merely approving of Rae, came to have a far warmer feeling for her. He liked his nephew, but strongly disliked his love-making; there was an impish light in Richard's eye that would have put any girl on her mettle, and the General's heart warmed as he watched Rae's calm, easy handling of the situation. He wondered whether she was in love—her face was not easy to read, and she was not a girl who said very much; the old man, glancing from her quiet self-possession to the handsome, challenging form of his nephew, found himself wondering where she got her coolness.

Lady Ashton watched with more uneasiness. She had, long ago, thankfully folded and put away the mantle of motherhood. She had found the role exacting but she had performed it, in her own estimation, faithfully. She had provided a house in which the children had enjoyed every freedom—she had sent them to the best schools and entertained their school friends; she had equipped them expensively and seen to their comfort. She had remained in England with them when she would have preferred to stay abroad with her husband. At his death, she had resisted her friends' urgings to marry again. Nobody had come forward with an offer of marriage, and Lady Ashton would as soon have thought of remarrying as of taking up tennis or hockey or any other of the strenuous sports of her youth, but she had remained a widow, and now felt that it had been for the children's sake. She had done much, but she was very glad to have to do no more. Their behaviour was something she always felt unable to control; each of the four children had what was beginning to be called a difficult temperament, and their mother felt that nothing could be done to change them. Estelle and Bruce had grown more satisfactory as the years passed, but Judy had never lost her regrettable tendency to insult those who bored her, and Richard—Richard was charming, but one had never been sure when he was serious.

Lady Ashton wondered whether he was serious now. It he was, it was a pity his eyes still had the look in them that had baffled her throughout his boyhood. If he was not, this extraordinarily public wooing must be causing Rae a great deal of discomfort. One ought perhaps to say something to him—to insist on more orthodox conduct. Lady Ashton had an uneasy vision of the discomforts of insisting, and decided to ask Blanche's advice. Blanche was sensible and clearheaded; she would know what should be done.

"What I was really wondering," said Lady Ashton, in the seclusion of Miss Beckwith's own sitting-room, "was whether Richard ought to go up and see the girl's aunt. They're her guardians, I presume, and they'll want to know something of the affair before the engagement takes place."

"That sort of thing isn't done quite so much nowadays," Miss Beckwith reminded her. "A great many girls live in complete independence—like Grace Mather's daughter, you remember. She had a flat in London, and Grace knew nothing of her engagement until an entire stranger called on her and informed her he was to be her son-in-law. You remember the one, don't you? He went down in the *Fleurette* some years later, poor fellow. Rae's aunts may have some control over her, but one doesn't really know. Has Richard met them?"

"No—I asked him. He knows that they're staying at the flat, but he hasn't met them. Should I speak to him, do you think? I could begin by asking if Rae's aunts had any objection to his paying her attention—no, that sounds too old-fashioned, I'm afraid."

"Much. As I say, these things nowadays are entirely the affair of the two most concerned. I don't agree that it is right—I think they want older and wiser heads behind them. Poor little Lady Gervaise used to say that she would never have got into such a hopeless tangle if her father had been alive at the time of her engagement. He would never have allowed that man in the house. What a dreadful fellow he was, Dorothy—do you remember?"

"Yes. You described him as flashy, and you were quite right."

"Yes. What a great relief it was when he went down in that Italian ship. They say he was the only British passenger on board, so it really looked providential, in a way. No, Dorothy, it's a pity, but I don't think you can say very much. If you talk to Rae, you might find that you embarrass her a great deal, and if you talk to Richard, he'll answer you with great seriousness and go on just the same as before. He's behaving exactly as he always behaved; one never knew how to take him and one never will. If Rae is to marry him, she can't expect other people to interpret his moods or his behaviour; she must come to her own conclusions. I'm sorry for her—at least, I would be if I thought she was really in love with him, but she's an unreadable girl and one can't really tell. The only help you could give would be to tell her whether Richard is serious or not—and she probably knows that far better than you do. You'd much better say nothing."

Upon this, it was decided to leave matters as they stood.

Judy was the only one who spoke of the affair to Rae. She brought Mr. Ferris over for the last sitting and, before driving away again, sought out Rae in the garden and opened with her usual abruptness.

"Where's Richard?"

"Cleaning the car," said Rae. "I've promised to go and watch him doing it."

Judy stared at her for a moment.

"Rae," she said, "what's going on? I mean, I can see what's going on, but I can't see where it's going to." She broke a twig off a nearby shrub and pulled it slowly to pieces. "I don't understand Richard—nobody ever did— but I thought I understood you, and now I find that I can't see through you, either—do you love him, Rae?"

"No," said Rae quietly.

There was a long silence before Judy spoke again.

"I see," she said at last. "Well—thanks. You're a nice girl,

Rae, and if he does anything to hurt you"—Judy snapped the twig viciously in two—"I'll—"

"I don't think he'll hurt me."

"You sound almost too sure."

"He hurt me once," admitted Rae. "When I came down here and you met me and told me that he wasn't here.... It shook me, but that was just what I needed. It shook me out of what I'd imagined was love. And it made me think, and it also made me take a clearer look at myself—twenty-one, sensible and level-headed, as a rule, but falling in love with someone who didn't seem to have quite the same feeling about me."

"But—"

"It wasn't pleasant," went on Rae, "but the point is that I faced it and it did me an awful lot of good. And when I say that Richard can't hurt me now, what I mean is that nothing—I'm sure—will ever be as hard to stand up to as those first few days I spent here. A thing like that doesn't seem to have much point at the time, but when the shock dies down a little, you find that you're left with a wariness —a—a sort of guard. You've been knocked down once but you can see that whatever it was that hurt you, doesn't hurt you any more. That's badly put, but that's how I feel. I like Richard; he's the sort of person a girl can't help liking, but most girls would have known that he was the kind of man you don't allow yourself to take too seriously."

During the silence that followed, Rae examined this reasoning and found it very sound. She had opened her heart too wide, and too soon; now she had closed it securely against

Richard's undeniable charm and appeal. She was glad to find that she could even acknowledge, with coolness and detachment, that he had great personal magnetism; this was a feeling, she told herself, that someone might have on handling a snake whose fangs had been removed, there was fascination, but no danger. No danger whatsoever.

"If you imagined you were in love with him," said Judy, "then I don't think you should have let a side-step in Rosanna's direction make any difference. People can be too forgiving; I thought when you took it so quietly—coming down and finding he wasn't here—that it meant you were going to let him off too lightly. But if you're going to write him off completely just because he got tangled up with Rosanna for a while, then I think that's almost worse than—than—"

"I didn't say I'd written him off, Judy. I said that I wasn't going to lay myself open to any more—shocks."

"Well, I'm all mixed up," said Judy. "I wanted you to like him a lot, and you did, and I was sorry. Now I want you to like him a little, and you won't—and I'm still sorry."

Rae smiled.

"Never mind about Richard," she said gently. "Can you-"

"Oh Rae!" burst out Judy, "can you believe that we sat over breakfast that morning so happily, full of plans and looking forward to his coming home? And now look. Richard proposing to you in broad daylight several times a day, and making everybody feel uncomfortable, and you taking it all with complete calm—and me stuck with that Edward ever since he came down here, listening to him struggling with one word at a time—"

"I like Edward," said Rae. "If you'd only give him a chance to talk—"

"A chance! I sit for hours and hours, just waiting for him to finish off a sentence!" protested Judy.

"But you frighten him. When he's not with you, he can be just as fluent as anybody else."

"The only time he's fluent," said Judy, "is when he gets on to his poems. It's odd, but he can sit and rattle those off without a hitch. You should hear him recite:

> *'Little Tommy Tucker*
> *Gave his nurse her supper*
> *Quantities of arsenic*
> *On brown bread and butter'*

By the time he's got all his poems worked out, he'll be a public speaker. Especially with me to practise on permanently."

"Permanently?"

"Practically," said Judy. "You know that empty flat on the same floor as ours? Well, he's taken it for the rest of his leave. So he'll be over every evening of our lives, reciting his nursery rhymes."

"I shan't mind," said Rae. "Will you?"

Judy shrugged helplessly.

"He won't mind whether I mind or not," she said." It's

funny, Rae—nothing gets through his skin. Nothing at all. When I give out a stream of directions—clear directions—as to how he can get away from me and stay away from me, he looks at me admiringly and says, 'How fluent you are.' He makes plans just as though I weren't there—he's drawn me pictures of the view from our house in a place with a frightful name like Wirraperropper or something equally darkest-Africa. He wants three boys and a girl, and he says his aunt'll come out and take care of them—she's good with children. He listens to me when I interrupt, and goes on from where he left off. He talks to all the Art students, and they think he's wonderful because he can sketch bull elephants or something better than they can. He's there all the time—whenever I look up, he's part of the landscape, outdoor or indoor. So you see it makes no difference having him in the flat opposite; if he hadn't taken it, he'd have moved in with us."

Her voice trailed into hopelessness, and Rae looked at her with a smile.

"By the way, Judy," she asked, "did you ever succeed in finding out what his surname is?"

"Yes," said Judy bitterly. "Leech."

Rae walked to the garage and, seating herself comfortably on an upturned box, watched Richard idly as he gave the final touches to the car. He looked up and gave her a friendly grin.

"Don't get too comfortable," he advised. "There's plenty

Men and Angels

to do; there's the windscreen and all the windows and all the inside."

"Go ahead," encouraged Rae. "I've lots of time to watch."

She found him pleasant to watch. He was absorbed in his task, and seemed to have lost, for the moment, his provocative manner. He was in his shirt-sleeves; there were smudges on his face, and his hair was disordered, giving him an unusually boyish look. He worked busily, saying little, but as the minutes went by, Rae found that the wariness which she wore as a shield during all their encounters was slipping from her, leaving her curiously relaxed. This was how she had always wanted things to be between them, she told herself with a stab of regret: quiet, pleasant and comfortable.

"Judy gone?" he asked after a while.

"Yes. I think she's rather tired of shuttling Mr. Ferris backwards and forwards."

"Won't be for long," commented Richard. What do you think of the picture?"

"I—I don't really know. I'm not really a judge."

"Of pictures?"

"Of anything."

"That's pretty sweeping, isn't it? I would have said that you'd done a good deal of judging lately. You've judged my character, for example, to be philandering, unstable, volatile, untrustworthy, and altogether unsubstantial—haven't you?"

"I don't think so. I haven't had that much time!"

He wiped his hands on a clean rag, threw it aside, and came over to sit beside her.

"I'd give a lot," he said, "to know what you really think of me—or if you ever do think of me."

"I used to." Rae smiled at him. "I used to think about you a great deal before I met you."

"Before you—"

"Before you came home. I lived with your photograph, you know. It was rather a good photograph."

"You can't go by photographs," said Richard. "They stay in their frames, for one thing, and never come to life. You can invest them with any kind of personality you like; you can even grow to depend on their steadiness of character. You can't blame them, can you, if they come to life and spring a few surprises?"

"I've never blamed you for anything, if that's what you mean," said Rae quietly. "Nobody's done any blaming—except perhaps Judy. Judy's a darling, but she's—she's impulsive, and she always says what she thinks. You'd be silly, and so would I, if we pretended that we hadn't known how anxious she was to—to throw us together, if that's what it's called. I don't suppose you wanted to be thrown any more than I did. But I enjoyed meeting you, and going out with you. I even enjoyed being made love to—or hadn't you noticed?"

"Yes, I've noticed."

"If you're really going to be honest," said Richard, "then

why not admit that you might have fallen in love with me, and stayed in love with me, if only I hadn't spent that weekend up in Town with Rosanna instead of spending it down here with you? That's really the trouble, isn't it?"

"I don't think there's any trouble—any serious trouble. I thought, at first, that perhaps you should have been here when I arrived, but that was because I was only looking at it from one point of view. There were others—such as the fact that Judy was down here, so that I wasn't being left entirely on my own. I didn't suppose—when I thought about it—that you'd really counted on spending the entire time down here with me!"

"Go on," said Richard quietly.

"And about Rosanna—"

"Well?"

"It's difficult to explain. It wasn't—jealousy I felt when Judy told me about her. It's something a man can't perhaps understand very well...You see, I know Rosanna pretty well. I had the room opposite hers for two whole years, and I know how she feels about things, and how she behaves—and that makes it hard for me to accept the fact that a man can get an equal amount of pleasure from my society and from—Rosanna's. I don't think my feelings were hurt, but I'm certain my pride was!—Is that honest enough?"

"You believe, do you, that an evening with you, and an evening with Rosanna, add up to the same thing?"

"I don't know. I only know that there are countless nice

girls in London—pretty, gay, amusing. You can meet them at any time. I know heaps of them, and you could take any one of them out for six days of the week and I'd be happy to go out with you on the seventh. That's the kind of competition I can understand and—and tolerate. But competition with Rosanna is something that I'd rather not let myself in for."

"All right, let's all be honest," said Richard. "I love you. The garage isn't the place to tell you so, but it's as good as all the other places I've had to say it in lately. I love you— do you believe me?"

"No."

"Then how do I get you to believe me? Do I crawl about looking submissive until my week-end with Rosanna fades out of your mind? Do I sign a declaration to the effect that it was a ghastly mistake and not to be repeated? Do I spend the rest of my leave struggling to get back to the kind of terms we were on when we were in London? If you love people, Rae, you have to take them on trust!"

"If you love them," agreed Rae.

"Look." Richard got to his feet and pulled Rae to hers. "I'm twenty-six, and for almost all my life I've been given a pretty free run. We all—all four of us—brought ourselves up, and I think we did it not too badly. Mother's not a disciplinarian, as you've probably gathered by now; we're all the walking, talking results of her system of letting things work out for themselves. You know Judy; you live with her, and you know that she's noisy, she's untidy, she insults people whenever she feels like it, she doesn't do a stroke of work, and she's completely and utterly self-absorbed. You know all that, but you manage to live with her and to like her."

"I—"

"Wait a minute. I'm her brother, and I've got all her charming characteristics and a few of my own thrown in. Why can't you apply to me—and to my failings—the same patience and tolerance—and love—that you show her? Why, knowing Judy, did you set a high standard for me? Why can't you allow yourself to see me as clearly as you see Judy—and still like me? I hurt you, Rae, and I'm sorry. I'm damnably sorry. I loved you and I hurt you, and— being the kind of man I am—I'll hurt you a good deal more. I'm sorry I made love to you in what you thought was a headlong manner. At least, I'm not sorry. Don't you know what you're like, Rae? Don't you? Coming home and expecting as I did, that Judy's friend would be a self-confident, sophisticated little piece like Judy—can't you see what effect you'd have? You're soft and sweet and terribly foolish and appallingly vulnerable, and you get round a man's heart and cling there so that he couldn't get you out even if he tried to. I know that I've got an insufferable manner and that I don't like people to know what I'm thinking or feeling—but can't you see what I'm thinking and feeling, even when I try not to let you? Can't you, Rae?"

She looked into his eyes and saw a trouble and a purpose she had never seen in them before. His arms were round her, and she found it sweet to allow herself to yield to them. She leaned against him, and in a little while felt his lips against hers and heard his whisper.

"Try to love me, Rae, my sweet!"

She had loved him, without trying. She remembered how swift and how easy it had been. But she remembered also the days and nights she had spent at his home on her arrival, lonely, bewildered and bitterly humiliated. She had come to Thorpe full of confidence in him and in her own heart and he had….

"Will you love me, Rae?"

She gave a tired little sigh.

"Oh, Richard I don't know! Once is enough...."

Chapter Fifteen

Thursday was wet, but Judy telephoned in the morning to say that she and Edward would come over to lunch. The students were to visit a beauty spot some twenty miles away and Judy would be free at the end of the morning.

The rain became heavy during lunch, and indoor amusement was plainly indicated. The four younger members made their way to the old playroom upstairs and, after trying several wireless programmes and finding themselves dissatisfied with each, switched off the radio and settled down to a large jig-saw puzzle depicting a country scene under an incredibly blue sky. Rae and Richard spread the pieces on the floor and began to sort them; Judy helped them, and Edward sat in a corner with a book of nursery rhymes and an expression of intense concentration.

It was into this peaceful scene that the General, putting his head round the door, dropped a bombshell.

"Telephone for you, Richard," he said.

"Thanks, sir. Coming." Richard stirred lazily. "Did you ask who it was?"

"Lady?" enquired Judy..

"Yes," said the General, doubt only too apparent in his voice.

Judy sat bolt upright and stared at her uncle.

"Did she tell you her name?" she asked.

"Yes. It was Lee. Miss Lee. Miss—I think it was Rosanna Lee."

There was a pause. Richard had sunk back into his lounging attitude against the sofa; Rae was moving pieces quietly; Judy was staring at her uncle with a frown on her brow. It did not need a more sensitive nature than the General's to feel the tension in the air.

"Well," he asked, with a touch of irritation, isn t anybody going to answer it?"

"We're awfully settled at the moment, said Richard with lazy calm. "You go, Edward."

"Me?"

"Yes. Say you've been all this time looking for me and I'm in my bath. Ask her to leave her number."

"But—"

"Go *on,*" commanded Judy. "And then you'd better put the car into shelter—it's going to drown, standing out there."

Edward rose obediently and followed the General out of the room. Richard went back to his task with a careless air, but Judy remained sitting on the ground staring straight in front of her. After a few moments, she got up restlessly and stared out of the window.

"The rain," drawled Richard, without looking up, "won't be over for hours."

Judy turned and addressed him thoughtfully.

"Richard—you're not going to ring her up, are you?"

"If I want to," said Richard evenly, "then of course I shall."

"Then I don't understand you," said Judy angrily. "I would have thought that that party would have shown you what she's really after."

"You know what she's really after?" asked Richard.

His tone was lazy, but Rae saw that he was no longer moving the pieces into position, and she was suddenly aware of where Judy's remarks were leading. The knowledge made her rise to her feet in an attempt to check matters before they went too far.

"Richard's teasing you, Judy," she said. "He's only trying to make you angry."

"He doesn't have to try," said Judy. "I only have to look at him to feel my hair standing up. He's going to wait until everybody's out of the way and then he's going to telephone to Rosanna to find out whether she's still having the success with Sir Fabian Hollis that she had at the party."

Richard, with great deliberation, fitted a green and blue shape into a tree outlined against a blue sky. This done, he got up slowly and dusted his trousers with care.

"Have you seen Rosanna lately?" he enquired idly through

the dusting.

"I haven't set eyes on her, thank goodness," said Judy, "since I saw her at the theatre doing her ridiculous act."

"She was disappointed," said Richard, "that you weren't at the party."

"She knew quite well that I wasn't going," said Judy heatedly. "I wanted to leave a clear field for you and that...that superannuated Casanova. Oh!"—she turned to Rae impulsively—"I didn't mean to—I'd forgotten... I'm sorry, Rae..."

Richard looked from one to the other, and spoke with a new note in his voice.

"You two," he said slowly, "seem to keep up to date. I didn't know Rae knew anybody of Sir Fabian Hollis's type. Do you know him well?" he asked Rae.

"Of course she does," said Judy. "If she hadn't told me all about him, I wouldn't have sent him to Rosanna's party."

Richard looked at her incredulously.

"You... What *is* all this?" he enquired coldly. "Are you losing your mind?"

"Please don't let's talk about it any more," begged Rae. "It's over and done with."

"It isn't by any means over," said Richard, and something in his voice drew her eyes to his face. He was staring at her with an expression in which astonishment and disbelief struggled for mastery, and she saw the suspicions that were slowly forming in his mind. His face whitened, and as they stared at one another, she felt her own cheeks redden with anger.

"Look, Rae—" began Judy.

"Wait a minute," said Richard. He was still staring at Rae. "There's something I'd like to know."

"There's nothing to know," said Judy. "I sent that invitation and—Rae, please let me do the talking—please!"

Rae turned to her and spoke gently.

"Judy—would you mind going away and leaving me with Richard, please?"

"With Richard, alone?" Judy's tone was one of stupefaction.

"Please, Judy. Just for a few minutes."

"No, Rae. All he wants to do is to ask you about Sir Fabian Hollis, and it's nothing—nothing at all—to do with him. I can explain—"

"Please, Judy."

Without another word, Judy turned and went out of the room, shutting the door gently behind her. Rae faced Richard calmly.

"You were saying—?" she said.

"Why did you send Judy outside?"

"You said there was something you wanted to know. If you want to know how Sir Fabian Hollis got to the party I can tell you."

"I don't care a damn how or why he got to the party. I want to know how it is you know a man of his reputation—you *do* know him?"

"Yes."

"You mean, you know him *well?*"

"Very well."

"Good God!" His voice was incredulous. "I don't believe it."

"It's true. I know quite a lot of people that you haven't heard about."

"A lot of people—perhaps. But not people like Hollis!"

She made no reply. She was surprised at her feeling of cold anger. He had told her that love and trust should go hand in hand—and he was standing before her with horror in his eyes and questioning her about...

"How long have you known him?"

"Do you think you have any right to ask?"

"If a man who considers himself engaged to you has any right to ask you what you know of a notorious rake like Hollis, then—yes, I have. How long have you known him?"

"I first saw him when I was about eighteen."

"Did you—go out with him?"

"Yes," said Rae calmly. "He arranged to send me to Madame Soublin's."

"S-send you to M-Madame—"

"Yes. I was in an office when he first met me, and he thought I was too young and—unpolished."

"My God!" He looked at her keenly. "Rae, are you telling the truth?"

"Yes."

"You mean that you actually took money—took money from—"

"Not exactly. It was Madame Soublin who took the money—as long as he paid it. But he didn't pay it for long."

"For—"

"Sir Fabian is good-looking, charming—some people think he's irresistible—but he has one great fault," explained Rae. "He's very mean where money is concerned. He promises, but he doesn't perform. He was to pay my fees for two years, but he—didn't. He was to pay part of the rent of the flat I share with Judy, but—"

"Part of the—good God!"

"—but he didn't. He was to have given me a dress allowance, but it didn't get paid more than two or three times."

"Dress...You took money from that—that—you took money for dresses—rent—"

"I'm trying to tell you. He promised, but he didn't pay."

"Did you...?" Richard was unable to go on, and Rae, guessing at what he could not say, felt a surge of anger that she had not experienced since the uninhibited days of the nursery. Every desire left her but the one to hurt as much as she was being hurt.

"I went out with him whenever he asked me," she said

with deadly calm, "but I never lived with him. He asked me to, but we—I refused. I didn't think he'd honour his debts, and I wasn't certain whether I should be held liable for them or not. So I went to live with Judy."

Richard walked to the window and stood staring out at the rain.

"Does Judy know this?"

"Yes."

He swung round and stared at her incredulously.

"Judy knew this! Judy!" He gave a short laugh. "I've been out of England too long," he said. "I was told about the new rules, the new freedoms, the—the new women, but I—I" He stopped and put an abrupt question: "Do you ever see Hollis now?"

"Sometimes."

"If I asked you not to go near him or to speak to him ever again, what would you say?"

"I should refuse," said Rae.

"That's all I want to know," said Richard.

He walked to the door, opened it and, passing Judy in the corridor without a word, went upstairs to his room.

Twenty minutes later he came downstairs with his suitcase and, passing his mother on the stairs with a brief word of farewell, left the house.

Chapter Sixteen

Dinner that night was far from cheerful. Miss Beckwith was the only one present whose mind was as easy as usual. Lady Ashton had told her that Richard had been called back to Town, but had said nothing of her uneasiness as to what had called him back. She would have liked to hear Blanche's comments on the situation, but was unable to decide whether there was a situation at all. Richard had said merely: "Goodbye, Mother, I've got to get back to Town." He had brushed her cheek with his lips in the usual way, and had gone. He had come suddenly, as he had often come and he had gone without warning, as he had often gone:' she could not in any way account for this feeling that all was not as it should be. If Judy looked tired, it was because all that driving was telling on her. Rae was pale, but it had been a wet day and she had had no exercise. It was absurd to feel uneasy. Lady Ashton, having come to this sensible conclusion, felt more uneasy than ever. Looking at Edward's serious countenance, she knew that he was as anxious as she was.

The General was in worse plight, for he knew that something was wrong. A girl of some sort had rung up and caused some kind of disagreement—the General was sure of it. Within half an hour of the call, Richard had flung himself out of the house and driven furiously away; Judy had undoubted traces of tears on her face, and Rae looked—the General swallowed a mouthful of spinach and came to the surprising conclusion that she looked like a drooping lily.

He refused more potatoes, waited for the chocolate custard, and came slowly to a decision. He would get hold of Rae after dinner and have it out with her. He would do the thing with the utmost delicacy, of course—but he had tackled delicate situations before. What could have been more tricky than that time old Swaine went off with that dreadful woman from—was it Pretoria or Philadelphia. Anybody with a heavy touch could have botched up the thing and got the whole affair into the newspapers. It took cautious handling, but he had been on the spot to handle it. Here was another case: Richard flung off, the girl left here looking absolutely peaked. Peaked. Piqued. There was quite a play on words there. He would get hold of her after dinner..

He had no difficulty in getting hold of Rae. Miss Beckwith went upstairs to tidy Richard's room; Lady Ashton followed her to have a talk; Edward went outside gloomily and polished Judy's car. The General, looking into the drawing-room, saw a desolate sight—Rae and Judy sitting staring out of the window in silent misery. He came into the room slowly, closed the door with care and cleared his throat.

"Herr-um. Cooler to-night," he ventured.

Men and Angels

There was no reply..

"More rain to-morrow, I shouldn't be surprised, said the General.

"Rae's going tomorrow," said Judy, without turning round.

"Eh?"

"Rae's going tomorrow."

"Tomorrow? You mean, you're cutting your visit short?" asked the General, turning to Rae.

She looked round and gave a little smile.

"If you don't mind," she said. "I've got an awful lot to do, and—"

"She hasn't anything to do," put in Judy wearily, "but she's had enough, and I don't blame her."

Rae rose slowly.

"I wonder if you'd mind if I went up to bed?" she asked her host. "It's been a—a heavy sort of day and—"

"You run up, my dear," said the General, putting out a huge hand and patting her awkwardly on the shoulder. "You run up and get tucked in and have a good night's sleep."

"Good night. Good night, Judy—will you be coming up before you go?"

"I'll look in," said Judy. "You go on up."

Rae went out and the General looked at his niece.

"Now, he said, "what's all this about? I don't pry into your business, as you know, but there's something going on—

there's something wrong. Is there anything I can do?"

"No," said Judy shortly.

"No what?" snapped the General.

"No, Uncle. No, sir. No, nothing. And don't expect me to be polite, because I don't feel polite."

"You don't know the meaning of the word," said the General. "None of you. I'd like to see what would have happened in my young days if a young cub turned up without notice and without a by-your-leave or with-your-leave, and then flung off again when his dinner was almost on the table. I don't look for politeness, young lady—I gave up looking for it a long time ago. Now what's all this fuss about?" he demanded.

"Rae's uncle."

"Eh?"

"I said Rae's uncle, Uncle."

"If your father were alive," said the General heavily, "I'd ask him to put you across his knee and keep you there till he'd got a little respect out of you. Who's Rae's uncle?"

"Rae's uncle, Uncle, is a gentleman called Sir Fabian Hollis."

"Good God!" exclaimed the General, causing Judy to sit up and look at him with the first sign of interest she had shown.

"Do you know him?" she asked.

"No, I don't. Don't want to. He's a member of my Club, that's all. Seen him, on and off, for years. Detestable feller."

"Yes. That's why Richard's pushed off."

"That's why what?"

"That's why Richard's gone."

"Why?"

"Because of what you just said."

"Because of what I—"

"Yes. You said he was a detestable feller. That's why."

The General found his hand itching, and did his best to suppress his rising anger. He eyed his niece, who looked back with a defiance behind which he could sense an unusual loss of self-confidence. He swallowed once or twice and spoke with surprising mildness.

"I wonder whether you'd have the goodness to tell me, he requested, "what the dooce Rae's uncle has got to do with Richard's departure."

"I can't tell you," said Judy wearily, "because I don't know. He's gone and can't explain, and Rae's here and won't explain. All I know is that he heard about Sir Fabian Hollis, and then they had some kind of argument, and then —well, he just went, that's all."

The General took his time to consider all the possibilities behind this meagre statement.

"Is there anything," he asked at last, "between Rae and Richard?"

"If there was," said Judy, "then there isn't now."

"Was there ever any—understanding?"

"Never. Just one long, hopeless misunderstanding practically from the start—that's all."

"Were they ever," pursued the General, exercising the greatest self-control, "in love with one another?"

"First she was, and he wasn't; then she wasn't and he was; now both of them aren't. I wish," said Judy, "that he'd stayed where he belonged, with naked savages, and left us to be happy without him."

She leaned back wearily and closed her eyes. There was silence, broken only by the General's breathing.

"Judy."

"I'm tired," said Judy.

"Judy!"

"I'm tired, *Uncle*. Sir, I mean."

"Judy!!!!" roared the General, in a voice that set the window curtains fluttering.

The effect was astonishing. Judy opened her eyes, sat up and burst into bitter tears. The General, awkward and flustered, balanced himself on the edge of the sofa and stared at her in dismay.

"Now, now, now," he said huskily. "There's no need to be frightened. You shouldn't work a man into a passion like that. I was only trying to get some sense into this tangle about Richard."

"I'm sick of Richard," sobbed Judy. "I'm sick, sick, sick of Richard. I hate Richard. I wish he was d-dead, the pig."

"Hush now, hush! There's no point in being abusive.

Dry your eyes and answer my question sensibly. Are they engaged?"

"No. Another day—just one more day and they would have been. I saw it coming," sobbed Judy. "And then this b-blasted uncle—"

"We're still at the wrong end," said the General. "How did it begin?"

"I began it. I b-began it and I f-finished it too," said Judy. "Ever since I saw Rae; I wanted her to—to marry Richard, because I didn't know what a pig he was. She says she doesn't love him, but she does—I know she does. She loves him. She loves him, the pig, oh, Uncle Bertram, the pig, the pig!"

"There now, there," admonished the General. "So you brought them together in London. And then?"

"And then Richard asked Rae down here, and she said she'd come."

"Why didn't he come too?"

"Because he went and met that Rosanna Lee."

"Do you know this woman?"

"She isn't a woman. She's a girl—she was at Madame Soublin's when we were, and now she's on the stage. She got hold of Richard, and so he didn't come down, and Rae was left high and dry without a soul down here to break the monotony or to make it bearable or anything."

"Quite so," said the General dryly. "And what made him come down finally?"

"Rosanna met Rae's uncle—he goes after actresses."

"I know."

"Well, I arranged for Rosanna to meet him at a party when Richard was going to be there I knew that if Richard saw the uncle making any impression, he'd leave Rosanna flat, and—"

"And it all worked out all right and he came down here, finished the General. "And you mean to tell me," he resumed after some thought, "that simply because Richard discovered that this feller is Rae's uncle—"

"Fine uncle," commented Judy bitterly. "Not a farthing towards her rent or her keep, and not a penny towards her school fees—after promising to pay them! A fine uncle! But how can a girl help who's her uncle?"

"It's very hard," agreed the General. "But wasn't there anything else? It's a pity the man *is* her uncle, but I don't quite see why that should cause Richard to—"

"Neither do I—but it *has,* you see. He went without a word, and Rae won't say anything, and she's going back to the flat. Her aunts are still there, but she says she wants to go back, and I don't blame her. I wish she'd never seen this place. I wish she'd never seen Richard. I wish—Oh!"

She broke off abruptly and, taking out a handkerchief, tried to repair the damage that tears had caused on her usually cheerful countenance. "It's Edward," she muttered. "I'll have to drive him back to Allbrook, and explain the whole thing to him and—Oh, I'm so *tired* of it all!"

The General gave her hand a pat, and Judy looked unexpectedly grateful.

"Will you knock on Rae's door," she asked, "and tell her I'll ring her up first thing in the morning?"

The General nodded, and made his way out of the room a few moments before Edward entered it. It seemed to the newcomer, at first, that the room was empty; then he caught sight of Judy's form by the window, and his face brightened.

"H-hello," he said, hesitatingly.

Judy, her back to him, made no reply, and Edward, watching her, sensed something vaguely unfamiliar in the poise of her head and the set of her shoulders. If it had been anybody but Judy, he would have said that she was depressed, but it was impossible to imagine Judy out of spirits. Accustomed to what other people termed her discourtesy but what Edward regarded as an enviable waywardness and lack of inhibition, he sat quietly on the sofa, waiting for her to take notice of him. An odd sound, however, and a movement of Judy's hand towards her eyes, brought him to his feet with an appalling suspicion filling his mind.

"I—I say," he asked. "You're—you're not upset, are you, about anything?"

"No, I'm not," said Judy.

"Oh," said Edward, relieved. "I—for a moment, I thought you were crying. Silly of me."

"Well, I'm not crying," said Judy, turning to him a face

upon which were the unmistakable marks of tears.

"Silly of me," he said again. He cleared some books from the sofa and patted it invitingly. "Good springs," he said.

Judy sat down. The spirit had gone out of her. Rae and Richard had quarrelled; Richard had gone away; her plans, her hopes for Rae—love, a home, money and freedom from care—none of them had come to anything. It was all over; there was only bitterness and disappointment. It was finished.

A tear fell slowly down, and then another. Edward stared at them, fascinated. After some time, it seemed that he had identified them, for he drew a handkerchief from his pocket and, shaking out its folds, handed it to Judy.

"Blow," he invited gently.

Judy blew fiercely and crushed the handkerchief into a ball in her hands.

"I'll drive you back in a minute," she said.

"Oh—no! " begged Edward. "I like to sit here and—"

It would be odd, he reflected, to say that he liked to see her cry, but he was experiencing a feeling of ease that he had not known since meeting her. This was not the cool, sharp-tongued young woman who ordered him about; this was a soft and tender creature who sat, tear-drenched, beside him, clutching his handkerchief in her hands.

"I say," he asked presently, "has somebody said something?"

"No," said Judy.

"Oh! If anybody *does,*" said Edward, "I hope you'll tell me."

The implication was clear. He would knock their heads off.

"Nobody said anything," said Judy, "but you may as well know. Rae and Richard"—she paused to steady herself—"they had a row, and he's gone—that's all."

"I see," said Edward, and sat thinking it over. "I see. But people do quarrel, you know. What makes you think—"

"I know," said Judy. "It's final. It's—he's gone."

"Do you know what they quarrelled about?"

"Partly. I wasn't there, but I'm pretty certain that it was—well, it was all connected with Rosanna."

"Oh—the telephone call."

"It was all my fault," said Judy, so forlornly that Edward put out a hand impulsively and laid it on hers.

"It'll all work out," he said. "You wait and see. These things do."

"Not this," said Judy, in a dead tone.

He looked at her anxiously, and strove to drive the look of despair from her eyes.

"You have to look ahead," he said, with less and less of his accustomed hesitation. "You know what they say about things being the same in a hundred years—it's perfectly true. They will be, only worse. Try to think about something else—if you cared to, I could show you a few more of the nursery rhymes for my book—would you?"

There was no assent, but, on the other hand, there was, as Edward noted with pleasure, no refusal. He took his notes from his pocket and sorted them earnestly.

This one, he said at last. "What d'you think of this?

Hickory, dickory, dock,

The mouse ran up the clock.

It happened to be an electric one

And the mouse fell dead from shock—or

The mouse got a terrible shock

—I can't decide which."

"Fell dead," said Judy.

"Yes I think on the whole..." *'Fell dead',* wrote Edward.

"Then there's this—it isn't complete:

Hush-a-bye, baby, on the tree-top,

When the bough breaks

Your Nannie'll go Plop!

But I don't think that'll really appeal to them—there's not really any violence there. I'm calling the book *Nursery Crimes,* unless somebody thought of it first and pinched the idea. What d'you think?"

"Does it matter what I think?"

"Oh—it matters a very great deal to me," said Edward seriously. "I can't really think of anything that matters more. More than you, I mean, Judy... I—"

"No," said Judy.

"You could get used to me," pleaded Edward.

"No," said Judy.

"You could *try*. Nobody can possibly know until they try, Judy."

"It's no use, Edward." Judy's voice was unusually gentle. "It's no use. I like people to be completely assured, and to have their minds made up about everything, and to have no hesitation about what they're going to do at any time or over anything."

"I shouldn't like a chap like that," said Edward bravely.

"You might not, but I—"

"You wouldn't like a chap like that, either. And if you did get hold of a chap like that—even if, mark you, you liked him—which you wouldn't, then even then he wouldn't be the chap for you."

"I can choose my own—"

"It's no use your getting hold of an assured chap," pursued Edward, "because it wouldn't do for two of you to be assured. Only one of you can be assured, and from what I know of you, it would be you."

"Naturally, I—"

"And if he had his mind made up about everything, at twenty-five or thirty or whatever age he'd be, then he'd be a pretty limited specimen by the time he'd reached forty or fifty, wouldn't he?"

"He could—"

"And hesitation, sometimes, isn't a bad thing at all. That old saw about he who hesitates being lost, doesn't cover the whole ground, by a long way. I know what you think of me, Judy. I'm not assured, and I only make up my mind when I'm pretty sure of my facts, and I hesitate all the time, especially when I'm with you, because I love you and that puts me off. But you could get used to me—I'm sure you could—if you gave it a chance."

"No, Edward, I—"

"You've never really given me a chance, so you don't know what I'm like. I'm not much of a chap, but I've got a good job and a better one in store, and I know it doesn't matter much, but I'll have a title some day, though there's no money with it. When you keep a chap at arm's length, you can't find out what he's like. You've never let me come near you like this or—"

"Keep off," said Judy.

"—or comfort you when you're feeling sad, as you are now. It doesn't hurt to have a shoulder to lean on—like that. It does you good and eases things a bit. If you'd relax quietly and let me stroke your hair—like this—which you've never let me have a chance of doing before—then I could have shared your troubles and taken some of them on to my own shoulders—Judy, are you comfortable?"

"I'm dreaming," said Judy.

"Just relax. I've got another one about Little Polly Flinders. Want to hear? Listen…"

⁂

The General, meanwhile, had given some thought to the matter of the quarrel between Rae and his nephew. Some judicious interference from somebody with an older, a wiser head, seemed to him desirable; after a short period of reflection upon how he should proceed to interfere, he went upstairs and knocked gently on the door of Rae's bedroom. After a moment, Rae, fully dressed and looking as though she was already on the point of departure, opened the door.

"I hoped you wouldn't be in bed," said the General. "May I came in and say a word?"

She nodded, and the General followed her into the room and stood by the window. Rae's suitcase was nearby, and he saw that it was packed.

"Have you made up your mind to go?" he asked.

"Yes, please."

"Well, I'm not going to try to keep you—that is, not for more than a day. But will you put it off for just one day?"

"But why?" asked Rae gently.

The General hesitated; he could hardly say: 'Because I've taken the matter in hand and therefore there will be no further mismanagement. I am going to Town to-morrow, and shall summon my nephew to lunch with me; I shall give him the benefit of my advice, and insist upon his returning with me so that you young people may settle your differences. I have keen judgment and a delicate touch, but I shall need a day; give me a day, and I shall give you my nephew.' Though he felt that the speech would be an effective and sensible one to make, the General found himself substituting a less effective one.

"Only just a day," he said with unusual diffidence. "I ask it as a favour. To please an old man, my dear—will you stay?"

Rae, trapped and helpless, could only smile.

"Of course," she said.

The General pressed her hand, said good night and went downstairs. The drawing-room wore its familiar look of peace; Lady Ashton was on the sofa with her cookery books, Miss Beckwith was looking a trifle sadly at the distance separating the dark man and the fair girl.

"I'm going up to Town in the morning, Dorothy," he said.

"To Town? I'll order the taxi, then. Eleven o'clock, as usual?"

"Yes. Don't forget the Duchess is coming to fetch the picture—it had better be left in the hall—oh, Rae's gone to bed—feeling a bit tired, she said."

"Has she a headache?"

"No, no—-she's just tired. I think I'll go up early myself," said the General.

"Do. You'll have a tiring day tomorrow, I expect," said Lady Ashton.

Chapter Seventeen

The General, waking on the following morning with his mind full of other matters, had entirely forgotten the Duchess and her exhibition, but Lady Ashton, meeting him in the hall, brought it to his mind.

"Before you leave, Bertram, I wonder if you'd mind putting the picture downstairs in the hall ready for the Duchess to take away?"

The General, muttering a sentence to the effect that he wished the Duchess would take it away and not bring it back, went upstairs and brought down the picture. He put it on a chair near the front door and gazed at it with dislike.

"Find me the likeness," he said aloud. "Just find me the likeness, that's all."

He turned and found, a little to his embarrassment, that he was not alone. Two small boys were standing in the hall, dressed neatly in grey flannel suits, red caps in hand.

"And who're you, eh?" he enquired with gruff amiability.

"We're Hugh and Alan Moore," said the older boy politely. "Good morning, sir."

"Ah! you're Rae's friends," said the General. "Come in, come in."

"Thank you very much, sir, but we can't stop. We've come to say good-bye. There's a car outside, and we're going back to school. We came to say good-bye to Rae."

"Well, I'll see where she is," said the General. "Sit down on those chairs—no, you can't sit down on that one, can you?—I've put the picture on it."

He saw that the boys were standing before the picture, looking at it with their heads screwed so far on one side that the General wondered whether they were going to turn over completely and view it upside down.

"Like it?" he enquired.

There was no reply. Both boys shuffled their feet and looked embarrassed, and the General beamed with gratification.

"Not impressed, hey?" he asked. "Well, you ought to be—that's been done by a tip-top feller who does all the people you read about in the papers. What don't you like about it, hey?"

"Those colours at the back," said Alan hesitatingly, "they look as though they've sort of run."

"That's what I think, too," said the General. "I think they've run round and round like the tigers in the story, till they've all run into one."

"I don't mind the colours so much," said Hugh, putting his head on the other side, "but that flower-pot isn't straight."

"Flower-pot, ha ha ha!" roared the delighted General. "Flower-pot, indeed! Now I'll show you what that flowerpot's really meant to be. Now wait a minute while I fetch it—I won't keep you, because I know you've got to be off, but you'd better see a good picture while you've got the chance."

He went upstairs and came down bearing triumphantly the Fitzroy. Lifting the other picture and placing it in the library, he placed his favourite work of art on the chair and pointed to it with pride.

"There's your flower-pot," he said. "The very same vase that you see there. One feller paints it as what it is a vase—and another feller paints it as a flower-pot. Just a question of how you see it, they tell me—well, which picture d'you prefer? One's done by this big feller, Aylmer Ferris, and the other one's done by my uncle, a feller called Fitzroy. Which d'you like of the two, hey?"

"This one," said the boys, with unhesitating sincerity.

Fine little chaps, thought the General, looking at them with pleasure. Good, clean, open-air types. Healthy and hard—and intelligent, too—intelligence sticking out all over them.

"Same initials," commented Alan, looking at the picture. "A. F."

"God bless m'soul, so they are," said the General. "Never struck me. Odd. Now I'll go and find—"

A commotion at the front door interrupted him. The Duchess, followed by a liveried chauffeur, was entering the hall.

She had discarded the polo topee, and was wearing a feathered toque which Hugh and Alan studied with undisguised wonder.

" 'Morning, General. Ah, you've got it ready, I see. Then we needn't waste your time or mine." She stepped back and half-closed her eyes, gazing at the Fitzroy. "Yes," she said. "The unmistakable Ferris touch—look at that brush-work."

"My dear Duchess," said the General, crimson with anger. "You're looking at—"

"I'm looking at it in a bad light—true," admitted the Duchess. "But I've got the very place for it up at the Castle. Who're those two boys you've got there? Oh, I know. The Farm. Why aren't you at school?" she demanded.

"We're just going," said Hugh, in a meek voice, wondering whether he ought to add 'your Grace'.

"Best place for you. Don't like boys roaming round when they ought to be safely in school. Come along, Peters," she ordered the chauffeur. "Lift it up carefully and carry it out."

"One moment," said the General.

"Can't possibly." The Duchess spoke with a touch of impatience. "Might have had time for a word if your sister'd been about—she knew I was coming, I presoom. Careful, Peters—careful, man!—Good-bye, General. Shall we see you up there this afternoon?"

"I'm afraid not," said the General. "I'm going up to Town. But allow me to—"

"Now don't keep me, General—I'm in a hurry. Goodbye

to you."

The General opened his mouth and then, with the remembrance of all he had endured from the Duchess, closed it again firmly. She had seized the Fitzroy and she was going to exhibit it; she was going to confront the students—to confront Aylmer Ferris himself—with the work, and point triumphantly to the Ferris touch. A vision of the scene rose before the General's eyes, and for a moment he wavered, but a thought of the insults he had endured stiffened him. She had held him in open contempt; she had used her sex and her position to expose him to his neighbours' ridicule. She had set herself up as a Patroness of Art. The General, giving praise where praise was due, felt bound to acknowledge that she knew a good painting when she saw one. He had tried to take the picture from her and she had informed him that she knew what she was doing. Well and good. Let her set it up before the students. Let her lead that feller Ferris up to it and show him what a vase looked like. It would open his eyes.

The General followed the short, stout figure down the steps and saw the Duchess into her car. Throwing back his shoulders and shedding the suppressed resentment of years, he walked up the steps into the hall and found two small faces uplifted to his. With a shock, he realised that the two visitors had been witnesses to the scene. Looking down at them, he wondered if he was imagining the calculating look in their eyes.

"Silly mistake," he said gruffly. "Have to telephone."

"You were quite right, sir," said Hugh, "to let her take it."

"It serves her right, sir," piped Alan. "She shouldn't have been rude."

"I tried to prevent her," said the General, slowly and distinctly.

"Yes, you did, sir, the first time," said Hugh. "We can tell anybody, when they ask us, that you tried the first time and she wouldn't listen. And so you just let her go on thinking whatever she wanted to."

"Yes. It serves her right," squeaked Alan.

"The whole thing can be put right in a jiffy," said the General. "Natural mistake, that's all. Now I'll see where Rae's got to."

"Don't bother, please sir," said Alan. "We're late, so if you'll please say we came, that'll be all right. And—and please, sir—"

He hesitated, and the General waited with an odd sense of uneasiness.

"We meant to ask you, sir," said Hugh, "about swimming in the river when we come home for the summer hols. We were wondering if you'd sort of mind."

"Just on hot days," put in Alan.

Good God, thought the General. Blackmail! At their age! He might have known it—he might have seen at once the signs of cunning on their faces. Low types. Distinctly low types. Juvenile delinquency written all over them.

"We're rather late, sir," said Hugh delicately.

Men and Angels

"Late? Well, what's keeping you?" asked the General. "You can be off, can't you?"

"Well, yes, sir. Will it be all right about the swimming?"

The General directed a fierce glance downward. Two pairs of eyes, limpid, innocent, stared back unabashed.

"Come'n see me when you get back," said the General.

"Yes, sir. It's very good of you, sir."

"Yes it is, sir. Thank you, sir. Good-bye, sir."

※

The General led Richard across the dining-room of his Club and made for a table near one of the windows. A waiter, hurrying after him, bowed and drew out a chair at a table set for two. The General seated himself, handed a menu to Richard, and looked round the rapidly filling room.

"Lot of strange faces," he remarked. "Shan't know the place soon—the usual for me. Richard, how about you? I can recommend the sole—it's always first-rate."

"I'd like something a bit heavier," said Richard. He gave his order and the waiter went away. The General helped himself to a roll, and, staring at it thoughtfully, wondered what had become of the opening phrases he had thought of on the train coming up to Town. How did they go? '—and speaking of marriage, my dear boy, there's something I'd like to say on that very subject...' But nobody was likely to mention marriage. 'I was sorry, Richard, to see you leave home so suddenly.' That was better. Then he could add a question as to what had caused the departure. It could be done towards the end of lunch, and he could say what he had to say and then lead the way out, giving the words time to bear fruit.

"This is very pleasant," said Richard, looking round. "We ought to do it more often."

"Don't get up much nowadays," said the General. "Your mother tells me you've been looking through the silver with her. Going to take any of it out with you?"

"No—it wouldn't be wise, sir. It's very well where it is. I had no idea how good the stuff was. There's some pretty fine plate—"

The talk went from domestic to national affairs, and the General, working through a solid meal and ordering coffee, found that he had enjoyed himself very much. The boy spoke well, he reflected, studying him. He had a good brain and he knew how to use it. He was a fine-looking feller, too —nothing weak and undersized about him. Good head, and a good physique. Pity he's made his home abroad—they needed more like him here. Well, wherever he was, he'd go a long way. He had looks, brains, breeding, and a good education—and he knew how to use them all. He was well on his feet; yes, firmly on. There wasn't a man in the room, young or old, who could give him points.

Looking round for one, the General's eye came to rest, and a look of distaste came over his face. Richard, glancing round, saw that his uncle was looking at a late-comer—a tall, well-dressed man who had paused to speak to a friend in the

Men and Angels

middle of the room.

"He's coming this way," muttered the General angrily. "Damned if he isn't going to take that table next to us."

The tall man passed them and paused. Richard looked up and met his eyes, and the colour drained out of his face. A waiter came up and pulled out a chair.

"Here, sir?"

"No, not this one." The voice was cultured, authoritative. "I'll take the one in the alcove."

"Very good, sir. This way."

He passed out of earshot, and the General gave a snort.

"Detestable feller," he said. "How d'you come to know him?"

"I don't really know him," said Richard coldly. "I came across him at a party a week or so ago. Do you know him?"

"Yes and no," said the General. "He's been a member here for years, but he keeps pretty well to himself. Got the reputation of being on the mean side, though I can't vouch for the truth of it. He never entertains here, at any rate. Odd how a man like that—he doesn't *look* a bad feller, after all—odd how he comes to have that streak."

"Streak?"

"Chasing women. I don't mean women of his own age—I'm talking of young women. I suppose you know he's always running after some young actress or other?"

"Yes, I gathered that."

243

"Well, it's a weakness, but men have their weaknesses," said the General.

He paused, struck by his subtlety. He had done that pretty well, he flattered himself. He had clean forgotten the possibility of the feller's turning up to lunch at the Club, and he had at once turned the circumstance to advantage. Not many men—the General stroked his whiskers—not many men could have brought off that neat beginning. The thing to do now was to come to the point. He cleared his throat.

"It's a pity," he said, with an air of frankness, "it's a great pity about Rae's connection with the fellow."

Richard, in the act of sipping his coffee, put the cup down and stared dazedly at his uncle. The expression irritated the General. This, he felt, was going a little too far. The girl had to have an uncle, and she couldn't be expected to control him. He might have been worse, after all.

"Connection?" said Richard after a time.

"Yes." The General frowned. "I take it you know of Rae's connection with that feller?"

"I—yes, I do. But I didn't dream that you did," said Richard.

"Well, I do," snapped the General, forgetting the subtle approach. "And while I think it's regrettable, I can't see why it should send you out of your mother's house without so much as a word to anyone. Apart from the discourtesy, I feel you—"

"Who told you?" broke in Richard.

"My dear boy," said the General, now thoroughly roused, "I didn't have to be told—I saw your car tearing up the drive and I—"

"Who told you about Rae and that fellow?"

"Who—oh! Well, it was Judy, as a matter of fact."

"Judy? You mean, Judy actually—"

"I don't say she would have confided in me," said the General, "because all you young people think that nobody ever went through anything but yourselves. You throw yourself out of the house like an—like an outraged lover in a melodrama, and leave that nice girl to eat her heart out, and you expect your mother and m'self to behave as though everything was going on as usual. Apart from being thoroughly bad manners, it's—"

"What did Judy tell you?"

"Judy," said the General, who was tired of being interrupted, "told me nothing. I extracted the facts from her, and I think, if you want my opinion, that you've behaved like a damned young puppy."

"What facts did you extract?"

The General looked with dislike at the handsome countenance before him. Good, he thought disgustedly, but no character. No real character showing. Signs—unmistakable signs of softness in that physique, too. Not a patch on any of the Fitzroys—he certainly didn't take after them, that much was certain.

"The facts of this unfortunate connection," he said. "Why you've come down so hard on the girl I can't for the life of me see. Do you deny that the feller's treated her abominably? Do you?"

Richard stared at his uncle, unable to speak. He had looked upon him, since boyhood, as the embodiment of rigid and unswerving uprightness. He had imagined that his views on what Richard termed that sort of thing were as fixed as they were unfashionable. And now, seated opposite, he was asking his own nephew to disregard—to blink at—to …

"Do you?" repeated the General. "I see you do. He promises to pay the girl's fees, and doesn't pay a penny; he allows her to work in a paltry job without so much as offering to keep her; he knows she's paying more rent than she can afford, and he makes no offer to relieve her of the burden. He—"

"Can I have a stiff drink?" asked Richard.

"Have anything you like," said the General, waving an angry hand. "But I must tell you that I think your attitude's damned unreasonable. Damned. Now that we're talking frankly, I'll admit that when your mother and I saw you with that girl, we were both of the opinion that she'd suit you down to the ground. She's a lady; what's more, she behaves like one. She's got the kind of looks that last, and she's intelligent. If all that won't do, then God knows what you want in a wife—I don't."

Richard felt better for his drink. He still stared at his uncle strangely, but the General was too angry to notice. He pushed the plates aside and, leaning on the table, addressed Richard earnestly.

"I came here," he said slowly, "to try to talk you into a more reasonable frame of mind. I'm not an interfering man, but I liked that girl, and I felt you'd never get one to suit you better. I never saw a woman I wanted to marry, at your age, but if I *had* seen one, I wouldn't have let a damned tailor's dummy like that feller there put me off."

"You wouldn't?"

"I most certainly would not have done."

"Well, you surprise me. In fact," said Richard, "for the first few moments, you took my breath away—need we continue the discussion, sir?"

"No, I suppose we needn't," said the General heavily. One look at the set face opposite was enough to tell him the uselessness of further discussion. The General, disappointed at the inexplicably unreasonable attitude his nephew had taken, looked about for a waiter.

"Catch that one's eye, will you?" he asked. "I'm sorry I wasted your time and m'own. But it seems extraordinary to me to think of some young hopeful coming after Judy and then changing his mind because he doesn't like the set of m'tie."

"The?" Richard looked steadily at the old man. He was beginning to talk a little wildly. Perhaps the heat...

"Yes, the set of m'tie," repeated the General. "Where's the difference? If the young men of to-day are going to marry the uncle as well as the niece, I'd better have a look at my own record."

"I don't—"

"—see the point. No, you wouldn't, when it involves someone else. I never, in all my life, heard such balderdash, and that's my last word—throwing over a girl because her uncle doesn't come up to scratch. Damned impertinence is what I'd term it, too. If any pretentious whippersnapper thinks I'm not good enough as an uncle, I hope he'll tell me to my face, that's all. Why don't you get up and go across to that feller now and say: 'I love your niece, but I can't swallow you!—Go on. No, I see you won't. Well, call that damned waiter and let's get out of here—what're you staring at?"

Richard's mouth had fallen open. His eyes, blank and fixed, were upon the well-groomed figure lunching in the alcove.

"I—I'd like a stiff drink," he said slowly.

"Have what you—what, another? Well, if you think it's wise—"

Richard ordered his drink and drank it slowly. Putting the glass down, he stared across the table, his eyes on his uncle, but his thoughts far away. He was back in the room at Thorpe, facing Rae across the abandoned jig-saw puzzle and seeing her face—calm, cold and steady. He went, word by word, over the exchange that had taken place between them, and knew that she had chosen her words deliberately to mislead him. He had entertained gross suspicions, and she had seen them and turned them, with cool calculation, into certainty. She had seen him storm away like a wronged lover, and had allowed him to believe that ... He had accused her, and she had had too much contempt for him to deny the charges. He had shown himself to be a fool, and worse. His face grew hot as he remembered his questions and heard her scornful answers. A clear picture of the figure he had cut came before his eyes, and he felt a chill creeping over him. He saw the General staring at him, and roused himself with a strong effort.

"I—I've been a—a bloody fool," he said bitterly.

"Quite agree," said the General. "Been trying to tell you so for the past half-hour. You're also an egotistical ass."

"That's true, too."

"And blown out with conceit."

"I think you're right."

"And blind. Blind as a bat. They ought to take fellows like you and exhibit them at shows."

"They do."

"Sometimes, just lately," summed up the General, "I've got to the point of wondering whether you're a man or a dooced monkey. But your own affairs are your own affairs and I wouldn't dream of interfering in them—get hold of that waiter and let's go."

Chapter Eighteen

The General left the Club seated beside his nephew in the car.

"You haven't much time if you're going to get me to Marylebone for the 3:30," he reminded him. "You'd be wise to do it through the Park."

He sat back, musing on his morning's work, not unsatisfied with the results. He had gained his point; though nothing had been said since lunch, he knew that Richard's attitude had changed. When they got to the station, he would go a step farther and urge him to return home. He would ...

"Look here," he said, rousing himself suddenly. "This isn't the way."

"Yes, it is," said Richard.

"Well, it isn't the way to the station. Where the devil d'you think we're going?"

"We're going to pay a call," said Richard, slipping neatly between two buses.

"Call? Call?" asked the General angrily. "What's this nonsense? I want to get back to Thorpe."

Men and Angels

"I'm going to drive you back," exclaimed Richard, "when we've done this. Now sit back and let your lunch digest."

The General, with a grunt, sat back. Richard drove the car into a side-street and drew up before a large block of flats.

"Judy's," said the General. "What the devil are we doing here?"

"I told you—we're paying a call."

"Well, you can go alone; I'm sitting here," said the General firmly.

Richard looked at him, and the General saw with surprise that there was something approaching humility in his manner.

"I brought you here, sir," he said slowly, "to see Rae's aunts. She thinks a great deal of them, and if I—if we could see them and explain something of the situation, they might give me some sort of message to to take back to Rae. I don't feel that I can go back after having made a prize fool of myself unless I can go back with some sort of—of backing. We could—I could tell them that I want to marry Rae, if she'll have me. If they thought it a—well, if they agreed, I could go back with some kind of—as I said, backing."

"You sound like that fellow Edward," commented the General. "And I'd like to say here and now that I don't understand you and never have. You've had us all acutely embarrassed for the past week and more; you've subjected an exceptionally gentle girl to a vulgar and humiliating courtship, if it was a courtship. I've watched you come and go without the smallest reference to anybody's convenience or feelings. You quarrel over a matter that seems to me to have been too trifling for anybody's notice, and fling yourself off without a word to anybody. And now you propose to go up there and ask the girl's aunts to conduct your affairs for you. When I was a young man, aunts weren't thought to be necessary at a time like this; a fellow behaved in a reasonable way and did his best to make a good impression on the young woman he wanted to marry. I've never known anyone who went this way about it before. You go out of your way to make the girl see you in the worst possible light, and then you come along here and ask her aunts to patch things up. This may be the modern way of—of winning and wooing, but I'm damned if I can see any point in it."

There was silence. Richard appeared to have no more to say, and after a time the General spoke again.

"I'll go up with you," he said, "on one condition."

"Well?"

"That you leave all the talking to me. Let me manage this affair for a change. All you've done is make a hash of it."

Richard made no demur. They went up to the flat, and were admitted by a tall woman, who introduced them to her sister and asked them to sit down.

"Is Rae all right?" asked Aunt Hester.

"Your niece is very well," said the General. "We called—"

"The name Fitzroy," broke in Aunt Anne thoughtfully, "is

a very familiar one—my sister and I knew a Colin Fitzroy. Are you by any chance related?"

"Old Colin? Great Scott!" exclaimed the General. "He's my first cousin—that is, if you're referring to the fellow who lived up near Wetherby."

"Our home used to be near there in the old days," said Aunt Anne. "We knew Colin extremely well. We always say he was brought up with us."

"But bless m'soul—the fellow's round about my own age," said the General in bewilderment. "Brought up with you—he must be a generation ahead."

"My father coached him—he came to our house when he was nearing his twenties, and he used to put us both in a wheelbarrow and shut us in the toolshed," explained Aunt Hester. "He came back year after year for many years after my father's death. We were very fond of him."

"He was a good chap, Colin," mused the General, lost in the past. "Pity about that—"

"Yes, that was an unfortunate marriage."

"You knew her too, did you?"

"My sister knew her better than I did—she was charming; but it was an unfortunate case of what's now known as incompatibles. They couldn't get on together, that was all."

"Yes—a shame. A great pity," said the General. "Wrecked his life, in a way. He stayed with me a good deal after his wife's death." He paused and, seeing Richard's eye on him, cleared his throat.

"Your niece is a very charming girl, if I may say so," he said.

Aunt Hester bowed.

"She's an unusual girl, too," went on the General. "She looks like one of the few who'll take advice from their elders."

"Young people don't need advice any more," said Aunt Hester calmly, "and my sister and I seldom give it. The most one can do is what we've just finished doing here—clearing up the mess."

"Those girls leave a mess?" enquired the General, shocked.

"Mess? It was some days before I could draw a breath without feeling that I was filling my lungs with the dust of years."

"Shocking," said the General. "Let my own house once, and made the mistake of not leaving the servants. Came back to squalor—I assure you, squalor. People of note, people of rank, people of prominence, they were, but I never thought the same of them after that. Squalor."

"That's the word I've been looking for," said Aunt Hester. "And the cobwebs in the kitchen—one can possibly excuse them elsewhere, but in the kitchen—"

"Great Scott! And girls like those, too. Well brought up, well educated. What do they teach them?" asked the General.

"Well, I—" began Richard.

"You may well ask," said Aunt Anne. "If you studied the literature in this flat, you'd think these girls never thought of anything but crime."

"Crime!"

"Extraordinary, isn't it? Rae tells me that they don't really read them—what does that mean, do you think?"

"Do forgive me," broke in Richard, "but—"

"You've got it looking pretty ship-shape," said the General, looking round with approval. "I've never been up here before, but I'm certain they won't recognise it when they get back."

"Would you like to look over it?" said Aunt Hester, rising.

"I'd like to, very much. Looks such a small sort of place for the enormous rent they pay."

Aunt Anne, left with Richard, looked at him speculatively. "I wonder," she said, "if you're any good at carpentry?"

"No, I'm not. Not a bit," said Richard firmly.

Aunt Anne was undaunted.

"There's a chair here," she said, rising and showing it to him. You'll find it hard to believe, but those two girls had left it with a leg off."

"Ah," said Richard non-committally.

"My sister and I tried to mend it, but it seems to give way—I think it wants some kind of reinforcing."

"No doubt," said Richard, rising as Aunt Hester re-entered the room with the General.

"Ah, I see you're just looking at the chair, Anne. Look at that chair, General. A leg off—and tied with a piece of string."

"Great Scott!" said the General. "String!"

"Mr. Ashton was just agreeing that it needed some kind of strengthening," said Aunt Anne.

"It wants a bit of wood there," said the General, bending to examine the damage. "It wouldn't take very long to put it to rights. If you had a few tools—but women never have tools," he ended, twinkling.

"I've got a hammer and some nails, and I could find a small piece of wood," said Aunt Hester. "But you mustn't—"

"Nonsense," said the General. "Won't take twenty minutes."

"It's too kind of you," said Aunt Anne. "But you must stay and have some tea afterwards."

"I'm awfully sorry," said Richard, "but you must count me out. I've got to—"

"Show them a piece of work nowdays," commented the General, "and they shy like mad. I wouldn't trust that young feller to drive a nail into anything. I wonder if I may take off my coat before starting on this? Thank you. I must talk to my sister about Judy leaving chair legs off without any attempt to have them put right. Tied with string, you say? Tck, tck, tck."

"Is your sister's name Dorothy, by any chance?" asked Aunt Anne. "Colin used to mention a Dorothy Fitzroy—would she have—"

"Richard's mother. Married a feller called Ashton and went abroad. Extraordinary, quite extraordinary," said the General, drawing off his coat and surrendering it to Aunt Anne; "extraordinary how one comes across people. Look here, Richard," he added, "if you'd like to go off, you needn't wait for me. I'd like to get this done and stay for a chat and some tea, but there's no need for you to wait—I can get back on the later train—no, bigger nails, I think. What other sizes have you there?"

"Well, good-bye," said Richard.

"Good-bye," said Aunt Anne, placing the General's coat carefully over the back of the sofa.

"Good-bye," said Aunt Hester, seeing him to the door. "How kind of you to come in."

"Not at all," said Richard. "My uncle insisted on my bringing him up to meet you. Good-bye."

Chapter Nineteen

Rae left the Lodge after lunch, followed by Bess, and walked slowly to the farm to say good-bye to Mart and Reeny. She missed the boys' boisterous greeting, and though she looked about her as she walked through the yard, she could see no signs of Bianca.

Mart was in the kitchen, looking unfamiliar in a plum-coloured coat and skirt and a formidable-looking hat.

"You're looking very smart," said Rae.

"This is my second best," said Mart. "I'm going to take Reeny and walk up to the Castle for the Exhibition. We don't want to see the pictures, but Reeny likes to get into the grounds and have a look at the flowers—d'you like me hat? Scotch berry—I saw the Queen in its dead spit in one of the papers the other day, on'y her feather went that way 'stead of this."

"It's very nice," said Rae. "Where's Reeny? I came to say good-bye."

"She's upstairs, titivating, but I wouldn't worry her with good-byes, ducks—it makes her feel sad. You're not looking too chirpy yourself. Feeling low?"

Men and Angels

"I'm going home to-morrow," said Rae. "It's a day or two early, but I wanted to—to get back."

Mart ignored this weak evasion.

"What's the trouble?" she asked bluntly. "Wouldn't be your young man, I suppose—he gorn off?"

To Rae's surprise and dismay, the simple question acted, without warning, as the key to the floodgates. They opened, and the pent-up excitement of weeks, the hope and disappointment, the confidence and fear, the ecstasy and the disillusionment melted and ran in warm trickles down her cheeks. She had no hope of stemming the flow; she sat on one of the hard chairs behind the kitchen door, her fists, doubled against her eyes, proving as inadequate as her small handkerchief to check the downpour.

Mart made no attempt at comfort. To Rae's relief she went quietly about the kitchen, laying a cloth for tea, getting tarts and cakes out of tins and arranging them on plates. After a time, she opened a drawer and, unfolding a large white piece of cloth, tore from it a generous square and handed it to Rae.

"There, dearie," she said. "Take that and have a mop up. It's not as good as a sheet, but it'll help. That's right and don't stop crying. Let it all come; let it all out and you'll be better for it. That's what I used to do—wash it all away. It's natural, and it's healthy. If pore Reeny had've done that, she'd have been all right, but she wouldn't—and she kept it all in, week after week, month after month, so of course it went to 'er 'ead. It has to go somewhere—'s only natural—what happened to your young man?" she asked, lifting a piece of pastry on to a dish. "Did 'e just walk off?"

Rae nodded. "But there was nothing—I mean, you mustn't think—"

"I don't think," said Mart. "I just use my eyes, and I used them when you first brought 'im 'ere. And I could have sworn he was up to 'is neck in love. Shows you can't always tell. How far had it gone?"

"Gone?" Rae looked up, surprised. "It hadn't really started. It was all just a sort of—a sort of muddle."

"Well, don't you sit down under it," urged Mart. "What I mean is, there'll be others. I used to dry my eyes and say, 'Mart, my girl, if you don't wipe away the eyedrops, you won't see the next one coming.' Men are just men, you'll find. When I married Joe Harris, I thought to myself, 'I've got one that's different'—but he wasn't, and we were happy in spite of it. From the time they're born, men get the best of it, and they make the most of it. If you start monkeying about and trying to change 'em, you get nowhere—you've got to take them as the Lord made 'em. You take my advice, dearie; try'n find one that'll stick to you, and if you find one that doesn't, have a good cry like you're doing, and wait till he comes back. With a pretty girl like you, you'll hardly get your peepers dry before the next in the queue'll step up, and when you're as old as I am, you'll find that they're all as like as two peas, under the top covering, I mean."

She chose a little cake from a plateful and carried it on a

Men and Angels

plate to Rae.

"Eat up," she said. "That and a glass o' milk and you'll wonder what you found in the bloke to cry over. He'll be back, likely as not, before you've got your eyes dry."

Rae left the cake while she went out to the sink and put her face into cold water. Returning, she made an attempt to restore the ravages made by the tears. She did not want the cake or the milk, but having forced them down for Mart's sake, found herself feeling better. She stood up and managed a smile.

"Thank you," she said. "I'm—"

Mart was not listening. With a shout of "Hey you, there!" she had seized an oven cloth and, dashing into the yard, was laying about her with a will.

"Go on, you—go on. Take that, you! Go on—in you go, all of you, in there. Go *on*, I said—ah, would you? Take that!"

The shouting, snarling and scuffling was muffled as a shed door banged. Mart reappeared, her hat askew, one hand clutching Bess by the collar. She dragged the animal in and banged the kitchen door behind her.

"You'd better hang on to 'er, dearie," she told Rae, "but it's not much good—it's too late."

"Too late?" repeated Rae in bewilderment.

"Yes. The deed's done. You'll catch it when you get home, I shouldn't wonder, but it's their fault—they oughter've known."

"Known?"

"Yes. And so should you, at your age. I'd get her 'ome, in your place, and keep 'er there—it'll be a puzzle of a litter, my word! I know for a fact that Nelson's got labrador in 'im, as well as bull-terrier and a dash of whippet. Blake's—well, nobody knows quite what Blake is, and Drake's related to most of the dogs this side of Thorpe."

Rae stared at her in horror.

"Is it—can't anything be done? They're so proud of Bess—they take such care of her and—"

"Well, she's a thoroughbred, you can see. You didn't ought to have let 'er hob-nob with this lot," said Mart. "You know what sailors are, dearie—you just take 'er 'ome and don't you say nothing about it."

"But—"

"When they get to know," said Mart, "you'll be safe in London. You just get 'er 'ome before those three sailor boys break out of that shed I've put 'em in. Listen to 'em! And you can't blame 'em, can you? I mean, dogs is only 'uman, after all—tell you what," she added, "you give 'er to me and I'll take her out to the yard—they've got a lorry there going down to the village—they can go past the Lodge and slip the dog into the garden, and then you won't be bothered with her—and they'll think she ran out on her own and got into bad company, see?"

"But they'll guess."

"Guessin's cheap," said Mart. "Now you come along with

Men and Angels

me, young Bess, and we'll give you a ride home."

"Good-bye, Mart—I hope I'll see you again one day."

" 'Course you'll see me again—I never saw such a pessimistic girl as you. You listen to me, ducks—that young man of yours'll be looking for you as soon as he's got over his little temper. Smile now—go on. Get a smile on your face and keep it there, men or no men. Good-bye for now. Next time I take Reeny up on a trip to see the lights, I'll bring 'er up to that flat of yours."

"Oh do—please! We'd love to see you, Mart! Good-bye, and—and thank you!"

She stood watching Mart going towards the yard. Bess, after some hesitation, followed her with dignity and every appearance of girlish innocence.

" 'Bye," called Mart. "He'll be back, see if he isn't."

Richard drove to the farm, left his car in the yard, and stood for a while looking about him. There was nobody in sight but Bianca, and he was not in the mood for listening to her lisping conversation. He went past her, going towards the kitchen, and Bianca jumped off the tree-trunk on which she had been balancing and skipped after him.

"Mart ithn't there—Mart's gone with Reeny to the—"

Bianca, in her eagerness to impart the information, tripped and fell headlong.

"There, there, there," said Richard, picking her up and

dusting her absently. "You're all right. Don't cry."

"I aren't crying," pointed out Bianca.

"That's right. Big girls never cry. Good-bye—I'm going to find Rae."

Richard strode on, and had gone four paces when Bianca's voice reached his ears. He pulled up and turned. Bianca, proceeding in a series of short hops, reached his side.

"What did you say?" he asked.

It was some moments before Bianca could understand that she was commanding attention. After a lifetime spent in piping down, shutting up, stowing it and putting a sock in it, she was being asked to repeat a statement. A grown-up stood before her, hanging with undisguised eagerness upon her words. Bianca drew a deep breath and, with a view to clearing the decks, removed a large peppermint drop from her mouth and placed it in the pocket of her dungarees.

"My canawy didn't sing when it was little," she began. "It didn't sing at all. It only singed when it was—"

"Fine, fine. Now tell me," said Richard, "where you saw Rae."

"I thaw Rae there"—Bianca waved in the general direction of the fields. "My canawy—"

"Is she there now?"

The golden curls shook vigorously. "No, she isn't there now any more. My canawy—"

"Yes, you said that. But *where?*" insisted Richard.

"There." Without turning, Bianca jerked one arm in a backward direction. "My wabbit had some little baby wabbits and—"

"Fine, fine—I hope they're all doing well. Now tell me where Rae went. Did she go *that* way through the lane, or did she go that way along there?" Richard's voice became urgent. He got down on one knee and took Bianca's hand in his own. "Now look, Bianca," he said, "you tell me where I can find Rae. I want to find Rae. Rae. Now will you tell me which way I can go?"

Bianca turned and pointed a small finger. "There, that way."

"Along that lane and through that wood?"

"Yeth. Near the pond."

To Bianca's intense disappointment, he rose and began to walk steadily up the lane. After a moment's dismay, she set off in pursuit. Running, stumbling, panting, she did her best to keep up with his long, purposeful strides.

"I'm coming too," she called. "Look at me Richard, I'm coming quickly!"

Richard, without slackening his pace, threw a glance over his shoulder.

"No, Bianca—go on home. Good girl. Good-bye."

He saw her come steadily on, and cursed under his breath. He lengthened his stride to shake her off, and hearing a howl of anguish, turned and saw that she was struggling to disentangle her curls from a blackberry bush. Cursing, he went back to extricate her, and spoke sternly.

"Now home," he said. "Go on—good dog—I mean—go home, Bianca."

He went on his way, resolved not to look round. A shuffling and a panting somewhere behind him told him that the pursuit was still on, but he knew he was setting a hopeless pace. He vaulted a gate and hurried towards the wood, and heard a yell that could not be ignored. He pulled up with a jerk, and turned. Bianca, scrambling through the gate, had got the seat of her dungarees caught, and was hanging, folded up, in mid-air. With a loud oath, Richard went back and lifted her down, putting her on her feet firmly.

"I told you to go *home!*"

"I'm coming with you to thee Rae," panted Bianca, getting a firm grasp on his coat. Richard moved on and Bianca moved with him, clinging tightly. She was sometimes on, sometimes off her feet, but the fierce clutch on the coat was never relaxed. Richard's opinion of children fell at every step, and at last he stopped and, picking her up, carried her along under his arm.

He found himself presently on the edge of a road. The wood had thinned, and before him was the pond of which Bianca had spoken. Looking round him, Richard saw the figure for which he was searching.

Rae was sitting on the grassy bank by the roadside, one hand pulling listlessly at the nearby tufts. Richard walked towards her, and as he came near, she looked up and met his eyes. He saw in hers the traces of tears, and without a word, went up and sat quietly beside her. There was no sound for a long time but the steady rhythm of Bianca's shoes scraping the ground as she swung to and fro on a gate.

"Rae," said Richard at last. He stopped and looked at her, his brow furrowed with worry. "You shouldn't have cried," he said.

"No," agreed Rae.

"Rae—I've nothing to say. I've been a fool."

"Both of us," said Rae. "Did the General send you back?"

"In a way. We had lunch, and Hollis came in and we—well, that was that. I'm sorry, Rae."

"It was my fault. I should have told you the truth. I mean, the whole truth."

"I should have known without being told—I went to see your aunts."

Surprise roused Rae.

"My aunts?"

"Yes. I wanted to tell them the whole thing and bring back some sort of message from them. I was even prepared to bring them back bodily. I wanted. ... I was afraid to come back and.... But your aunts and my uncle got on to Colin Fitzroy and Dorothy Fitzroy, and after that he took off his coat and prepared to mend the chair—and so I came back." He put out a hand and drew her to him. "Do you love me, Rae?"

"Yes, I do," said Rae.

"And always will, in spite of anything I may or may not do?"

Rae sighed gently.

"And always will."

"My darling. .. . You've got such soft lips...."

There was a long silence, and then from behind came a triumphant cry.

"Look—I'm thwimming!"

"Quick, Richard, quick! The pond," cried Rae. "Wade, darling, wade...."

The Castle grounds stretched for many miles beyond the vast, gloomy building, but a rope had been placed across the drive, and two footmen were on duty to inform visitors that their shilling's-worth took them no farther. They might look at the terraces and the lawns, but they must keep out of the Park.

The Art students, standing about in disconsolate groups, wondered why they had come. They had been bidden by a Duchess, but their hopes of entertainment had died in the chill of their reception, and even the thought of the collection of Art treasures inside the Castle failed to rouse them.

Mart and Reeny, paying their shillings at the gate, strolled about without any of the restlessness which moved those who had had no previous experience of the Duchess's hospitality. It was a pleasant day, and they were content to enjoy a distant

Men and Angels

view of the Park and a closer one of the interesting-looking students.

There was a stir in the Castle doorway, and the Duchess came on to the terrace, followed by two or three members of her staff.

"Where's Mr. Ferris?" she asked sternly. "He's keeping everybody waiting. Where is he?"

There was no sign of Mr. Ferris. The Duchess turned to a footman with a word of command, and he hurried indoors to obey.

"Now, everybody inside," she commanded. "Come along, come along; up the steps, everybody. Hurry, please—hurry!"

She turned as the footman returned, and held out her hand.

"Give it to me," she said, "and go along and see that everybody comes inside at once."

Mart stared for one horror-stricken second at the thing the Duchess was holding and then, with a choking cry, started forward.

"Excuse me, your Grace—"

The Duchess gave her a stony glare.

"Out of my way, my good woman," she ordered. "Oh—there's Mr. Ferris. Come along, come along, Mr. Ferris—we've been waiting for a long time. I was just about to ring a bell to summon everybody. Is anybody else out on the lawns there? Perhaps I had better ring."

"Your Grace," implored Mart earnestly, "I—"

The Duchess ignored the interruption. Raising the bell, she shook it vigorously, and the terrace resounded to a loud unmusical clanging.

"Now then," she began.

"All in line, all in line," screamed a parrot-like voice. "All in line there—go along."

The students, after one glance, went along. Reeny got them into a straight line and surveyed them with a keen glance.

"You boy, there—back—that's right."

"How dare—" began the Duchess in a terrible voice, and stopped abruptly as Reeny advanced upon her.

"Into line—and you," said Reeny, waving towards Mr. Ferris. He took the arm of the paralysed Duchess and urged her towards the line.

"That's right," said Reeny. "No—put the little girl in front—she's the smallest. Now—attention! Mark time, left right, left right, left *right*—feet *up* nicely, feet *up,* left right, left right, left turn!"

The line turned. Mart, looking round wildly, saw a familiar grey coupé drive slowly past the iron gates, and raised a hand in desperate summons. Thankfully she saw the car swing into the entrance and approach rapidly.

"Left, right, all together, left right, left right, now inside, boys and girls, quick march. Left, right...."

The boys and girls, led by the Duchess, marched into the Castle.

Men and Angels

A bell had rung at almost the same moment at the Lodge. The General came out of the library and walked across the hall to answer the telephone.

"This is Sheafton Abbott 4," he informed the caller.

A familiar voice came over the wire.

"This is Miss Lee speaking. Miss Rosanna Lee," it informed the General. "Can I speak to Mr. Ashton?"

The General's moustache quivered. Lifting the receiver from his ear for a moment, he stared at it as though it had been a snake which had bitten him. Replacing it against his ear, he summoned his fighting spirit. If she thought she was going to disarrange everything just when he had got it shipshape...

"Mr. *Richard* Ashton?" he asked, playing for time.

"Yes." There was something peremptory in the tone which stiffened the General. Would she, by Jove? Not if he could do anything. No, b'Jove. He gave a defiant snort.

"Is that you, Richard?" cooed the voice.

"Eh? No. This is General Fitzroy speaking—Mr. Ashton's uncle. Yes. I'm extremely sorry, but Mr. Ashton has gone to Kenya. Yes.... No, he was called away....Yes, extremely short notice indeed. ... I beg your? Oh, where can you get hold of him? His address is Care of Post Box Number three hundred and—What's that? Oh, the name of the *ship!* Oh no, no, no— he went by air.... Yes—oh yes, he must be half-way there by now. I'm so sorry.... What's that?—Oh, good-bye."

The General replaced the receiver and stroked his whiskers. Humming a little tune, he went into the library and shut the door.

THE END

The Friendly Air

By:

Elizabeth Cadell

"Why do you have to? It's your father's problem. If you do manage to persuade her to come to London instead of going to York, how do you know she won't get into your hair instead of his?"

"She has no claim whatsoever on me. I suppose you could say that she hasn't much claim on my father either, but she's always held him responsible for what she calls her disastrous mistake in leaving Edinburgh and burying herself in a bleak Yorkshire village. She said she did it on his advice—and so she's felt entitled to badger him ever since on every matter, big or small, that she wants cleared up."

For the first time, Emma's interest quickened. She hung the drying-up cloth on a hook, slid back the concealing panel and turned to look at him.

"Advice? You mean it was simply because he advised her—"

He frowned.

"You don't listen. I've tried to make it clear that she's not a woman who'd take anybody's advice."

"But she did take his advice about leaving Edinburgh and coming down to York?"

"Yes, she did," he answered, gratified to find that she was at last evincing some interest in the subject. "It was about the only occasion on which she listened to him. But that's all ancient history. The only thing that concerns us now is to prevent her from—"

"You don't like talking about the beginning of it, do you?" she broke in. "Why on earth not?"

"Because I see no reason to rake up an episode that shows my father in a rather unfavourable light. It was all over six years ago, and—"

"I know that. What I'm asking you is what happened before it was over."

"I don't want to discuss it."

Her patience splintered.

"Well, I do," she stated. "I'm sick of the way you've always skated around the topic. Six years ago, your father made a fool of himself. So what? Old men frequently do. I was eighteen at the time, an age at which you'd suppose a girl could be told some of the more sordid facts of life without swooning, but all I got out of my grandfather was the bare fact that your father had remarried. The village talked, of course, and I had good ears. I listened to all I could."

"Then you probably got a completely garbled version."

"I probably did. So ungarble it. Tell me the terrible truth.

Unveil your father's shame."

"*Shame?*"

"As you said, garbled. How can you get any help from me in this affair if I am not put into the picture?"

He hesitated.

"Very well," he said at last. "I'll tell you what happened, but I shall not, now or in the future, allow you to—"

"—wallow. Mud, mud, glorious mud. Go on—tell me the worst."

"There was no worst. It was simply a case of a man of mature years losing his head over an attractive young girl"

"Where did he meet her?"

"In Edinburgh. He and I went up from York for the Edinburgh Festival. I was twenty-eight and working, as you know, in my father's firm of lawyers. The hotels in Edinburgh were charging what he considered inflated prices, so he was pleased when a friend of his told him about a lady—an elderly lady, English, widow of a Scottish baronet—who had a large house in Edinburgh and was prepared to receive one or two guests for the period of the Festival. Screened, of course."

"Of course."

"I resent your tone, and I don't like your insinuation that my father's a snob. He—"

"—just likes carefully screened people round him. Do go on," she urged impatiently, "and leave out the unessentials."

"After an exchange of letters, my father and I went up.

It wasn't at all what we'd hoped to find. The house was quiet enough, but it was extremely uncomfortable. There was only one maid, and the food wasn't up to much."

"Cheap?"

"It was very expensive, but then — "

"I forgot. Scottish baronet's widow. So?"

"I went to concerts. My father preferred to go to plays. If our tastes had been similar, if I'd been with him more than I was, if he—"

"You sound like Kipling. Shouldn't the heroine enter at this point?"

"If you persist in—"

"Where was this attractive young girl?"

"Staying in the house—the only other guest. She was Lady Grantly's great-niece."

"How attractive?"

"She was rather small, very pretty, and had auburn hair. Her name was Morag."

He paused and brooded, and she went to join him at the fire. Reluctantly, he moved his chair an inch or two farther away from it, and she brought a footstool and sat at his feet. This was the time, she mused, when couples coupled—united after absence, warmed and fed, with coffee bubbling at the end of its electric tail. This was the moment for him to seek response from her relaxed body. Who wrote all those books and plays about characters jumping the matrimonial gun?

she wondered. They'd never met Gerald. But even if he did decide to jump, he wouldn't dream of jumping in this room, which acted on him like an extinguisher. And while his cousin Claud continued to entertain a succession of women in the flat they shared in Chelsea, he couldn't jump there either, so she was probably fated to be that despised and derided commodity, a virgin bride—and she rather liked the idea, she decided, though she wouldn't have cared to admit it and risk being looked down on as under-sexed, instead of being looked up to as over-sexed. There didn't seem to be a norm.

"Was this Morag sexy?" she inquired.

"I suppose you could say so. She certainly tried to engage my attention."

"You mean she chased you?"

"If you care to put it like that, yes. I don't have to tell you that I was of a serious turn of mind."

"And still are. Then what?"

"The concerts took place at night. During the day, I went round Edinburgh, which I had never seen before, and which I found extremely interesting. It's history—"

"I'll read it up. You went to concerts, your father... How old was she?"

There was a pause.

"She was seventeen," Gerald answered reluctantly at last.

"Seventeen!"

"And a half."

"And your father was fifty-nine. And a half. You were right about mature years. It makes you think of those medieval marriages. What on earth could she have—"

She stopped, "—seen in him?" Why ask? He was her godfather and she knew the answer, and knew very well what a sexy seventeen-year-old would have seen. Tall, well-preserved, handsome, with crisp grey hair, blue, quizzical eyes, a kindly manner. He looked like an archdeacon —which was probably why he had chosen to retire to an historic little house in the very shadow of York Minster, a layman in an ecclesiastical setting, discreetly wealthy, respected, pitied for that brief episode during which a scheming girl had taken advantage of him.

"Go on," she prompted. "You were enjoying the concerts and didn't see what was going on. But where was the great-aunt? Where was the Scottish baronet's widow?"

"Lady Grantly was never at home. If you believed her, she was running the Festival single-handed. That left my father and Morag together, and nobody knew the first thing about the affair until they announced that they were engaged and were going to be married without delay. You can imagine my feelings!"

"Never mind your feelings. Proceed."

"They were married in Edinburgh, and then they came back to York, to my father's house—which by that time I had left."

"Weren't you at the wedding?"

"I was not. I wasn't even in York when they got back. That was when I transferred myself to a firm of lawyers in London. The marriage lasted four months. Then she found a younger man and went off with him. My father felt nothing but relief."

Humiliation too, Emma thought. He wouldn't have enjoyed the role of deserted husband.

"So how did the great-aunt, Lady Grantly, get to Yorkshire?"

"She made more fuss over the affair than all the other relations put together. She said that my father had ruined her position in Edinburgh. The parents were very well-connected and influential, and she said that they blamed her for everything. So my father advised her to sell her house and live near York. He arranged the sale of her house and found her a cottage in Oatfields, which as you know is unfortunately only thirty miles from York. She's been there ever since, and she probably wouldn't dream of leaving if this money hadn't gone to her head. As it is, she decided to buy a house in York, and picked out one next door to the one my father's been settled in so comfortably for the past two years. She was nuisance enough when she was thirty miles away, but if she comes to live next door, he'll have to move. He couldn't stand it. That was why he appealed to me—to us—to try and persuade her to find a house in London instead. And that was why I spent a freezing week-end up there, achieving exactly nothing."

"She couldn't have been poor before she got this money. Didn't you say she owned a large house and — "

"Too large, and completely out of date. It sold very badly. Her husband hadn't left her much—that was why she supplemented her income by taking in occasional guests. My father advised her to invest the proceeds of the Edinburgh house, but before he could advise her what to buy, she'd made her own decision and bought a packet of Terrazone shares—a tin mine God only knows where. She gave some of them to my father and his wife, but they weren't worth the paper they were printed on. My father advised his wife to sell them at once."

"And she did?"

"Yes." He made the admission reluctantly. "She did. Two hundred shares in a tin mine which turned out...Two hundred shares which would have sold a month ago at...What the hell's the use of thinking about it?"

"Is Lady Grantly crowing?"

"No. She's too busy making plans to move. If you'd gone up with me, we might have talked her out of it. You could have met her as my future wife, we could have said we hoped she would consider moving to London instead of to York, we could have explained that we ourselves would soon be house-hunting and would put her in touch with any houses that might suit her. But you wouldn't come, and so she's still fixed on York."

"What exactly did you say to her today?"

"Nothing. She doesn't wait for anybody to say anything. She began, as I told you, by pretending not to recognise me. She went on to make disparaging remarks about my father. When I mentioned my engagement, she said that you had obviously not consulted the cards."

"The what?"

"Cards."

"What did she mean by that?"

"God knows. I didn't ask her—I didn't know how tangled it might get. She told my father that the cards had put her on to Terrazone. You see what I mean by being cracked? She was odd enough when we first met her, but I daresay her great-niece's marriage, her great-niece's subsequent elopement and her own recent lucky streak have all added up to send her over the edge."

"What's the house in Oatfields like?"

"Small, bleak, stuffed with furniture, most of it rather good. I would have liked to buy a couple of pieces. In fact, I suggested it—and wished I hadn't. She—Are you listening?"

'Yes and no. I was thinking."

"Thinking about what?"

"Going to see her."

For some moments, he was unable to speak. He turned in his chair and stared at her.

"Going to... going to...What the hell does that mean?"

"I thought I'd pay her a visit while I was up in Yorkshire, that's all."

"That's all? That's all? After having refused to go—"

"Don't let's go over all that again. Use your head. For years, you and your father have shied away from any mention of Lady Grantly. As it was nothing to do with me, I didn't mind how much you shied. But now you've got me interested. Put it down to your gifts as a raconteur. You've turned her from a dim and rather dull figure into a real person, and I'd like to see her, even if it's only to ask her what she meant about the cards."

"And you couldn't have come with me?"

"No. Anyway, all you wanted me to go for was to bully an old woman and—"

"Bully?"

"Persuade. Advise. Bully."

"Look here, I've had enough of this. I'm going."

"You haven't drunk your coffee."

"I don't want my coffee. This is the kind of thing you're always doing—refusing to co-operate, keeping well out of a thing, and then coming in at the last moment by a side door. To go and see her together"—He rose and jerked his coat off the hook on which he had hung it— "would have been reasonable. To profess interest now, to insinuate that you can do more on your own than my father and I have done... And anyway, you're too late. You'll be wasting your time. Goodbye. If I stay, we shall have a row, and if we have a row, I shall say things I don't mean."

"No you won't. You'll say things you do mean. —You've got a bit of pie on your blouse."

"Would you kindly—"

"Sorry. Shirt. I wouldn't put that scarf on, if I were you. It's damp."

He crumpled it up furiously and thrust it into his pocket. He opened the door, backed away to allow an old lady to cross the landing on her way to the bathroom, and turned for a last word.

"When are you going up?"

"On Wednesday. I'll be back on Saturday, unless there's a snow block."

"And you're serious about going to see Lady Grantly?"

"Serious? I thought it might be amusing."

"Amusing is the last thing you'll find it. I can't think why the hell you want to do it. What have you and she in common?"

Emilia did not tell him.

End of preview.

To continue reading, look for the book entitled:

"The Friendly Air" by Elizabeth Cadell.

About the Author

Elizabeth Vandyke was born in British India at the beginning of the 20th century. She married a young Scotsman and became Elizabeth Cadell, remaining in India until the illness and death of her much-loved husband found her in England, with a son and a daughter to bring up, at the beginning of World War 2. At the end of the war she published her first book, a light-hearted depiction of the family life she loved. Humour and optimism conquered sorrow and widowhood, and the many books she wrote won her a wide public, besides enabling her to educate her children (her son joined the British Navy and became an Admiral), and allowing her to travel, which she loved. Spain, France and Portugal provide a background to many of her books, although England and India were not forgotten. She finally settled in Portugal, where her married daughter still lives, and died when well into her 80s, much missed by her 7 grandchildren, who had all benefitted from her humour, wisdom and gentle teaching. British India is now only a memory, and the quiet English village life that Elizabeth Cadell wrote about has changed a great deal, but her vivid characters, their love affairs and the tears and laughter they provoke, still attract many readers, young and not-so-young, in this twenty-first century. Reprinting these books will please her fans and it is hoped will win her new ones.

Also by Elizabeth Cadell

My Dear Aunt Flora
Fishy, Said the Admiral
River Lodge
Family Gathering
Iris in Winter
Sun in the Morning
The Greenwood Shady
The Frenchman & the Lady
Men & Angels
Journey's Eve
Spring Green
The Gentlemen Go By
The Cuckoo in Spring
Money to Burn
The Lark Shall Sing
Consider The Lilies
The Blue Sky of Spring
Bridal Array
Shadow on the Water
Sugar Candy Cottage
The Green Empress
Alice Where Art Thou?
The Yellow Brick Road
Six Impossible Things
Honey For Tea
The Language of the Heart
Mixed Marriage

Letter to My Love
Death Among Friends
Be My Guest
Canary Yellow
The Fox From His Lair
The Corner Shop
The Stratton Story
The Golden Collar
The Past Tense of Love
The Friendly Air
Home for the Wedding
The Haymaker
Deck With Flowers
The Fledgling
Game in Diamonds
Parson's House
Round Dozen
Return Match
The Marrying Kind
Any Two Can Play
A Lion in the Way
Remains to be Seen
The Waiting Game
The Empty Nest
Out of the Rain
Death and Miss Dane

Afterword

Note: Elizabeth Cadell is a British author who wrote her books using the traditional British spelling. Therefore because these books are being published worldwide, the heirs have agreed to keep her books exactly as she wrote them and not change the spelling.